PRAISE FOR THE WRITING OF
JANE PALMER

'Jane Palmer's novel is a real find – definitely a specimen of higher lunacy. How characters quite as insane as these turn out to be as plausible as anyone you'd find in the average bus-queue, I do not know; but one time or another I've met all these people.' **Mary Gentle**, *Interzone*

'Delightfully witty, blending farce, black humour, a strong thoughtful plot and rich characterisation into a gourmet novel. Excellent.' *SFF Books*

'The "familiar" voice – if there is one – should surely be credited to Jane Palmer, who . . . has more in common with Muriel Spark than Marge Piercy. Her alien invasion of Earth takes place among the kind of people who cause havoc at the supermarket checkout. With deft comedy, she creates a Feminist who's literally the size of a planet . . . daunting.' **Jane Solanas**, *Time Out*

'Like a fresh sea breeze, blowing away the lingering clouds of intellectual fog, emotional steam and the smoke from the verbal pyrotechnics.' **Lee Montgomerie**, *Interzone*

'Hilarious.' *SFF Books*

JANE PALMER is one of the most original writers in fantasy and science fiction today. She achieved widespread critical acclaim with her witty and fast-moving novels, *The Planet Dweller*, *Moving Moosevan*, and *The Watcher*. Here, in *The Drune*, her most ambitious book yet, she brings together a delightfully "Palmeresque" combination of eccentric characters, classic science fantasy and her inimitable sense of fun.

Cover illustration by Dandi Palmer

THE
DRUNE

To Pamela,
With Best Wishes,
From Jane.

31. 8. 99

Also by Jane Palmer in Science Fiction

THE PLANET DWELLER

MOVING MOOSEVAN

THE WATCHER

THE
DRUNE

JANE PALMER

SWIFT
PUBLISHERS

THE DRUNE

A Swift Book

First published in Great Britain by Swift Publishers 1999

1 3 5 7 9 8 6 4 2

Copyright © Jane Palmer 1999

The author asserts the moral right to be identified as the author of
this work

A catalogue record for this book is available from the British Library

ISBN 1-874082-27-8

Typeset at the Spartan Press Ltd,
Lymington, Hants
Printed in Great Britain by
Caledonian International Book Manufacturing Ltd,
Glasgow

Swift Publishers
PO Box 1436, Sheffield S17 3XP
Tel 0114 2353344; Fax 0114 2620148
e-mail: enquiries@swiftpublishers.com
Website: www.swiftpublishers.com

"We're all mad here. I'm mad. You're mad."
"How do you know I'm mad?" said Alice.
"You must be," said the Cat, "or you wouldn't have come down here."

Alice's Adventures in Wonderland, by Lewis Carroll

To the memory of Ros de Lanerolle.

1

A crack appeared in the iron-hard permafrost. A couple of reindeer looked at each other to make sure it was nothing to do with them. The crack deepened and the couple padded away to find less active pasture. They didn't bother to turn and see the massive, black diamond teeth break surface to get their operator's bearings, then vanish just as rapidly again. They probably knew that it was impossible to burrow through permafrost at that speed. At least that would be what the unfortunate commander of the plundered missile base would duly protest, later . . .

"Pulled through a shaft chewed out of solid granite?" the general repeated in amazement. "Nothing on Earth could burrow at that speed."

"Nevertheless," his *aide-de-camp* faltered, "the shaft is still there, though obviously the lower part of it must have caved in under the pressure shortly after it happened."

"What about the Other Side?"

"It's now taken four of their multiple warheads as well."

"A matching set, then!" The general leant back. "We'll

have to maintain a news blackout. At this rate we won't have anything left to negotiate arms reductions with. Have Security turned up any suspects yet?"

"They're getting little co-operation from the police. They want to know what it's about."

"Tell them we've had intelligence that there's a plot to burrow into our gold reserves. If they think bullion's involved that will gee them up."

"Right, sir. When are we going to tell the President?"

"Which one?"

"This country's, sir."

"Oh, him! His advisers know. Let them do it, but better make sure the Kremlin knows. Don't like the thought of the Russians finding out before we get round to telling them. They've been a bit touchy since we cancelled that joint scheme for a cometary missile."

The *aide-de-camp* laughed. "Can't make them out. How often do they think comets assume a collision course with Earth?"

"Must be something to do with the one that flattened Tunguska." The general tossed his pen onto the desk. "With the number of satellite signals blocking astronomical observations we probably wouldn't know about it until it was too late anyhow."

The *aide-de-camp* pondered on the crater in good old Arizona, the state where his mother lived, and hoped Superman was up there somewhere watching.

Walton once again lifted the chalk in an attempt to put the final touches to his diagram explaining the Doppler effect, but it wasn't to be. From beneath the Hertzsprung-Russell diagram of main sequence stars, a thin voice, like that of a thoughtful mouse, piped up.

"If the Galaxy is throbbing with life, why is it so unlikely to pay us a visit?"

At that moment Walton's powerful fist would rather have been raised threateningly at the bright art historian who decided her students' horizons should be widened by lectures on astronomy. It didn't help to know that his group of mathematically minded pupils was enjoying her drawing instruction more than his customary chemistry classes.

"We are hardly on the route to anywhere important," he assumed his most charismatic smile to explain. "For the inconvenience it would cause another civilization to come here, the return would be very small."

"But that's supposing they only know as much as we do. If there are so many life forms out there, at least some of them must know how to get here in a couple of days."

"That depends on the length of their day, and anyone with technology that advanced would more than likely dismiss us as we would a microbe."

Why couldn't these dotty, plastic-spangled pupils have the same docile outlook as his own brain stormed students? They got their kicks from small, uncontrolled explosions and misaligning computer space bars with war games. Walton decided that art was not good for the stability of the human psyche if taken as seriously as equations. Though had he voiced the sentiment, one of this motley crew would have been bound to point out that nobody had ever been blown up by the iconoclastic power of a work of art. He may have had the authority of middle age, a second class honours degree and several diplomas in physics, chemistry, mathematics and all the esoteric stuff, and have been built like Ataturk's tomb, but there was no way he could intimidate this class of free thinkers. At times Walton wished he could have erased all reference to the sixties; they had to be generating their ideas from somewhere and their usual teacher wasn't even old enough to have been influenced by the seventies. It was probably something that happened to the young once they had managed to live without television for a day and removed their Walkmans.

Through his annoyance, Walton could hear a quiet voice from the back of the class.

"My Uncle saw a UFO."

The voice clearly belonged to a girl and so he hoped he could intimidate her out of the delusion.

"Has he any proof?"

"Took a picture of it." Poppy admitted reluctantly. She had not intended him to hear the revelation.

"Yes," joined in a chorus. "It's a good one."

"Where is it?"

Poppy shrugged. "Here."

"On you?"

"Yeah."

"Can I see it?"

"He wouldn't like that."

"Why not?"

"He don't like scientists. They made him move off his old farm so they could test some weapon."

The girl's persistence fired Walton's curiosity. "If he's got proof, surely he would like to have it confirmed?"

"Says he don't care what the poxy scientists say. He says that the UFOs don't bother him, so why should he bother them?"

"If he were right . . ."

"He is. That's why he don't want to be bothered."

"Show him the photo, Pop," her bespectacled friend insisted in a plummy accent. "We don't want the Doc to think we're wasting his time."

"I won't bother your uncle even if I do think it's genuine," Walton assured her, wiping the elegant logic of Doppler and Hubble away with one stroke of the eraser.

"Oh! All right." Poppy pulled a much folded and thumbed photo from her purse.

Walton reached over several spiked hairdos to take it. A cursory glance at the evidence made his professional cynicism waver. He was compelled to swallow hard. He had often had cold and clammy nightmares about this moment. His third wife had put it forward as one of the reasons for divorce.

"It's very good," he commented too casually to be convincing. "Have you had it analyzed?"

"What for? We know it's real."

"You were there when it was taken?"

"I saw the marks where it landed."

"Where was this?"

"I ain't saying."

"All right." Walton handed the photo back, as if disinterested. This Poppy was a tough little blossom so he indulged in a little elementary psychology.

"They don't bother him, and they've locked folk away on the say-so of people like you," she added defensively.

"Not me. I'm an astronomer, not a Witch-Finder General."

"You've spent half the morning telling us we're nuts if we believe in flying saucers," protested one of the more vocal factions.

"All I was implying is that it is possible for wishes to be converted into a sort of reality when one is not aware of the different things these sightings can be attributed to."

"What if Pop's Uncle Arthur is right though?"

"I can't compel Poppy to talk about it. She isn't obliged to prove anything to me."

"Why don't you phone him, Pop?" rose a chorus. "Show Dr Clarke he's wrong."

"He wouldn't like . . ."

But the timid girl was soon overwhelmed and Walton silently said "hooray" for elementary psychology.

2

Janice turned the television off. "What are you thinking about darling?" she asked for the fourth time.

Aware of what could exasperate a wife, and particularly wanting to keep this one, Walton raised his thoughtful gaze from the road map. "I'm trying to fathom the quickest route to Green Willow Farm."

"Why?"

"Because I don't trust those two dotty art students to drive me there in their clapped out buggy."

Janice experienced a faint hope that her husband's dedication to logic might at last have begun to mellow. "You're not taking up sketching are you?"

"No. The uncle of one of them took a very convincing photo of a strange aircraft."

"You mean an unidentified flying object?"

"It was obviously airborne and a craft of some sort, but if I manage to track it down it will not be unidentified."

"Well, do be careful all the same, dear."

"You don't really believe in those things as well, do you?"

"I don't know – you do talk about them quite a lot in your sleep. Two nights ago you were orbiting Uranus in a spaceship."

"You should have woken me up."

"Why?"

"There's more action on Venus."

"You're working too hard."

Walton sat back. "Am I?"

"What else?"

"What do you mean?"

"I sometimes wonder if we're living on the same planet."

He stared at his wife. "Why?"

"Your mind's always wandering off. I wouldn't be surprised if you had an alternative existence somewhere else. You should slow down before you really do start seeing UFOs. I can't afford to have you put away just yet."

Walton knew what Janice meant, but didn't want to admit it. It wasn't the students getting to him, but life in general. He was fifty and hadn't even managed to get some small asteroid named after him. Soon he would be too old to visit observatories at the top of the Earth's breathable atmosphere or South Pole where he could discover some rogue comet or be savaged by a Weddell seal. It was all downhill from now on, he reflected despondently.

Walton gazed at his wife as though she were some point in the distance.

"What is it?" Janice demanded. "Don't you like this dress?"

"Must be hormones."

"Yours or mine?"

"Is all this real?"

"It was when I got up this morning, but I have the feeling someone's going to turn into a pumpkin before midnight."

"Why doesn't the Universe make more sense? How could it all have exploded into existence from nothing?"

"Fax God for an explanation."

Walton ignored her. "How do we know it's real? I

sometimes get the feeling that the molecules in our minds are conspiring against us."

"It's probably your age, dear."

"Thanks." Walton didn't like to be reminded that he was twelve years older than his wife.

"We all have that feeling at some time or other."

"Why?"

"What do your mean? Why?"

"Why should we? It doesn't serve any evolutionary or self-protective purpose."

"It doesn't seem that odd to others because they don't have brains like logicians. There is such a thing as a romantic imagination, you know."

"What's romance got to do with it?"

"Look, if you're going to be a pain!"

"No, really. Why should anyone be regularly struck in the face with the wet fish of futility?"

Janice sidled down onto the arm of his chair. "Those daft kids have been giving you a rough time, haven't they?"

"I keep thinking they know what it's about."

"So that's why you're going to hunt UFOs at Green Willow Farm?"

Walton carefully folded the map. "I'd feel happier if I could prove them wrong."

"I always suspected you were a kill-joy." Janice went to the table and started to clear plates away. "Your turn to do the dishes."

"I've had a heavy day. You stack them in the machine and I'll mow the lawn later."

"It'll be too dark and you might get carried off by a UFO."

Walton chuckled. "Would it bother you?"

"Of course. How would I prove that to the insurance company? At least your other wives ended up with alimony. We can't even afford an *au pair*."

9

Walton stretched. "Oh well, you make enough to support the both of us."

There was a clatter as Janice loaded crockery into the dishwasher. "And buy presents for your brats."

"Oh spare me! There hasn't been a birthday for months."

"Maybe not. Suppose I'll have to buy you a present instead."

"Why?"

"You're fifty tomorrow, darling." Walton groaned, but she didn't hear. "Don't forget the party." Walton groaned even louder and she came back in. "Helen's bringing the poodles as well. You'd better do the lawn before you go out tomorrow – you know what Genghis Khan is."

"If we hadn't already agreed to separate, I would have divorced her over that animal."

"That was his sire."

"What?"

"Attila was the one who used to go for your ankles. Genghis is his son."

"I've always suspected that she bred them to attack me."

"Stop whining. Helen's the only one who wouldn't take money from you when the marriage broke up. If she hadn't given you a loan you wouldn't have been able to marry Lettice."

"They were both mistakes. Neither of them really understood me."

"Women usually divorce their husbands because they do. What wife wants to understand the principal of receding galaxies and the possibility of the ion drive at two o'clock in the morning in a warm bed? Look what you did to Lettice. She must have been a happily dim girl before you married her."

"But that was an innocent experiment."

"You knew she was dim when you married her and should have been happy with the arrangement. That woman had enough sex drive to launch Apollo. But no, you weren't satisfied, were you."

"But I thought it was for the best."

"What on earth made you play her tapes, explaining how to cope with every mathematical problem thought up since the pyramids, while she slept?"

"It didn't do any harm."

"Well, since she took up that professor's chair of higher mathematics, it's improved her prospects no end. I don't suppose she earned much as a manicurist. Served you right, you big blob. You should have known your ego wouldn't have been able to stand the competition."

Walton took the mug of coffee Janice pushed at him. "I wish you women wouldn't get on so well together. It gives me the feeling I've been passed around."

"So what are we meant to do? Fight for you?"

"Might seem more natural."

Janice laughed. "Oh come on, Walton. Meet the twenty-first century. Women don't need to fight over men any more. Stop living in the past."

"My ego needs the break every now and then."

"I just worry about you when you're late home or go on some bizarre field trip."

"You're probably more worried about me treading on the wildlife."

She ruffled his hair. "Well don't frighten any little green men you may run into tomorrow. We shall probably need to get on good terms with the rest of the Universe sooner than we think."

3

Akaylia Jackson wondered why she could never find a hole accommodating enough to let her through, so she could make some more interesting geological discoveries. Even a fifteen stone, middle-aged poet deserved some breaks from life. Tucking her tattered map back into the wallet commemorating a lifetime of failed romances, she breathed deeply and pushed until either the basalt or her bottom had to yield. The wallet erupted from her waistcoat pocket and littered the darkness below with photos of her lost loves. They had all talked too much anyway, besides claiming special privileges because of a midget chromosome. She concentrated her effort on saving her shawl and satchel of tools. If she wasn't able to chip herself out of the crevice she was going to need to keep warm until rescue came. After promising herself to diet for the twentieth time, her flesh eventually relented and released her back into daylight.

Akaylia was certain that there must be a way into this extinct volcano's fumaroles. Cursing in rhyming couplets, she pecked at the implacable pumice with her pick. It had swallowed her boyfriends, now in return it might have presented her with a fissure large enough to accommodate her backside.

Hunger pangs persuaded Akaylia to stop and break her promise about the diet. Munching her way through her last sandwich she gazed over the deserted landscape. There were the usual trees, grass and a few flowers, of course, but it was hardly a National Park. Even her pet passion, that stubborn volcano, was not esteemed by any others to be worth the chippings that she regularly brought back from it. It would never elucidate the theory of continental drift or point the way to a gold mine, but Akaylia was a dewy-eyed romantic as far as rocks were concerned. They could tell you the history of the world without having to utter one word – or would do so if you could get at them. Let the ambitious find their oilfields and intellectuals their proofs and theories; what would they produce but more pollution and more words. Let them poke around Surtsey and Kilauea, but Akaylia had the feeling that this was the place. Once inside those volcanic depths she knew she was going to find wonders they would never encounter.

Something white bobbed through the long grass below her. An albino deer perhaps? But deer did not wear bright red tartan waistcoats, not even in the rutting season. For a short while all she could make out was a mop of snow-white hair and the vivid suit. Akaylia supposed it to be bipedal and moving fast because it intended no one should see it.

Tiring of its excursion through the grass, it turned back to the volcano. Akaylia knew every unyielding inch of that natural structure. The creature may have been half her size, but it was not likely to have had access to any nooks and crannies she did not know about. Feeling irrationally protective towards the volcano, she decided to follow it. Perhaps the government wanted to cart the thing away for landfill and he was surveying it for them. She was sure there were better ways of discovering its composition. Nobody was going to lay violent hands on her volcano.

Stealthily Akaylia descended, trying to keep the bobbing

head in view. With a quick cautious glance about and flurry of red tartan, its owner disappeared beneath an overhang. She had cornered it. That led nowhere. Shawl streaming behind her, she bounded down and was just in time to see the obsidian wall beneath the overhang moving. With an accuracy in throwing a grappling iron that she had learnt at potholing classes, she hurled her satchel into the crack before it could close. Something crunched loudly, probably her thermos flask, but the gap remained. Not stopping to wonder what manner of tribe lived beyond it, Akaylia eased her shoulder against the slab and started to push. There were occasions when her bulk came in useful. The obsidian was no match for it and groaned open.

Beyond a dark stretch of passage was a complex of illuminated corridors. Spotlighted at their junction and staring at her in disbelief was a small man. He stepped aside in alarm and fell off the narrow path. After retrieving her satchel, she carefully picked her way towards the accident.

"Are you all right little fellow?" she called tentatively into the darkness below.

"No!" an irritated voice snapped back. "I've twisted my ankle." The white hair appeared from the gloom.

Akaylia grasped the extended hand and, with careful ease, pulled its owner back onto the path. Then she inspected the bundle of annoyance in amazement. He was wittering curses in an unrecognizable tongue and glared back at her.

> "Wonder of wonders to ever be true.
> I am Akaylia. What are you?"

"I'm called Rabette," he snapped.

There could have been no place on Earth where this splinter of humanity, or herbivorous mammal, would have seemed inconspicuous. Lack of exposure to daylight must have been responsible for the total absence of pigmentation

14

in his skin and hair and, quite possibly, his height of less than five feet. Why someone with such a startlingly bleached complexion should have decided to wear vibrant red tartan trousers and waistcoat was a mystery.

Even after the murderous tumble he had taken, Rabette seemed more concerned about his hair than his injured ankle or the rhyming interloper, and vainly combed it back into place with his fingers. As the fine fluffy thatch was as tightly curled and luxuriant as her own, Akaylia could hardly see what was wrong with it. Nevertheless, she handed him her large-toothed comb, so he could carefully tease out some tangles until he was satisfied the cotton white locks were correctly arranged.

"You don't seem very keen on visitors, little snowflake? Or are you an optical illusion planted by omnipotent powers to keep mischievous mortals away?"

Rabette gave the large black geologist a penetrating glare. "No," he said.

"I would offer to leave you in peace, but your ankle may not appreciate that."

"We don't allow visitors in here. Unfortunately the entrance is controlled by a time switch."

"A mechanically bolted burrow for a very rare robotized rabbit."

"I'm not a robot!" he snapped.

"Sorry. Figure of poetic licence. What are you then?"

"I'm not telling you."

"A hibernating herbivorous hermit." Akaylia looked at the regularity of the tunnels. "A megalomaniac motorized mole. An anthropoid alien acquaintance of Alice"

"I'm not an alien."

"Ah!" Akaylia sighed. "A neurotic non entity not necessarily of nature's intention."

He could see that she wasn't going to give up. "You would probably call me an Atlantian."

"I was afraid I might."
"We sank with our continent."

"In the best possible tradition.
Humanity has a second edition."

"Despite what you prissy geologists say, we did once have a continent."
"Not so much as a petty protest passed my pursed lips.

"If the flight of the bumble bee must be true,
What's to stop me believing in you?"

Then something more immediate occurred to her. "What happens now?"
"Anyone who manages to find their way in usually stays. You are going to be very conspicuous though."
"Even if I pull in the paunch and bleach the bonnet?"
"With skin that dark? It would look very odd. You really are a problem. Perhaps I should give you a memory erasing drug and let you out when the time lock opens the entrance."

"I refuse to be fobbed off so easily.
It's taken me years to find a way in here.
Now I'm going to look around, my precious little dear."

"Have it your own way." Rabette shrugged. "I don't suppose it matters that much any more."
"Why not?"
"Hardly any of us left in here. I'd sooner live outside anyway."

"What? With your absence of suntan?
I've seen more colour in a vanilla meringue."

"I could educate my dermis."

"I could teach mine to sing the Stars and Stripes. Forget it, little Munchkin. We live at opposite ends of nature's shade-card. This place doesn't have any food, does it?"

"A few hours in here and you'll soon lose your appetite."

"You underestimate the urgency of my digestive juices. If provoked, they could break down jute matting."

Rabette believed her. "Well I hope you're a vegetarian."

"I eat anything. Why?"

"There are no animals down here."

"Why not?"

"They've got better sense."

"What is down here then?"

Rabette smiled artfully, knowing what sudden drops to vast depths would do, even to her digestive juices. "How far down do you want to go?"

"Show me continental drift – from underneath."

"All right." Beckoning her to follow, Rabette limped off.

Slinging her satchel over her shoulder, Akaylia ambled after him until they came to a large shutter in the floor. Rabette pushed a button on its rim. The shutter opened to reveal a tunnel. Its sides were padded all the way down but fell away steeply for so far it was impossible to tell where it ended.

"You came up that?" Akaylia gasped, more apprehensive about going down it.

"Only way in and out. Used to be a ventilation shaft, but I worked out the air pressure needed to take my weight."

"What about my weight?"

"By the time you reach the bottom you'll probably be kilos lighter."

"Now look, little egg white – !"

"It's not wide enough for a capsule. Anyway, there would be hell to pay if the others found out I regularly came up here. Just follow me." With a knowing smile, Rabette leapt into the centre of the hole.

Akaylia watched as his white locks rapidly shrank to a small dot before disappearing completely. Normally, there wasn't much that would make her hesitate, but plummeting down bottomless shafts on nothing more than a cushion of air did give her pause. She removed her shoes and pushed them into her satchel then tied her shawl round her thighs to stop her skirt blowing over her head; as it was a once in a lifetime experience she might as well see where she was going. She sat on the lip of the hole then, taking a deep breath, pushed off.

Travelling as fast as Newton's apple, Akaylia passed lights, fossils, marble, granite, coal seams, gold seams, other tunnels and some very intriguing wall carvings, until eventually she hit the pressure barrier Rabette had activated to brake her fall. Her shawl spun off and her voluminous skirt reared over her head like a mauve poppy bursting angrily into flower. Rabette never even noticed her arrival. He had believed she wouldn't have the nerve to follow him.

Collecting her shawl and her dignity, Akaylia ambled into a large strange room that had the faint aroma of the seaside.

4

Green Willow Farm was one of the most featureless places Walton had ever seen. Bland acres of a single crop, hardly broken by a hedge, spread out from the road leading to Uncle Arthur's equally humdrum chalet bungalow. Walton couldn't help wondering what improvement war games had made to *his* old farm.

A squawk of starlings swung on the solitary telephone line, only to explode into flight as the car approached. At least this island in the ocean of nodding yellow had a phone. Even Walton would have felt intimidated at the thought of meeting the owner of this bleak prospect without giving him prior warning. Uncle Arthur did have the intelligence to operate an SLR camera though, so perhaps he was viewing the old man in an unfair light. Poppy and her up-market friend, Bryony, seemed so convinced of the man's benevolence he should have been reassured.

The first living creature they set eyes on was Uncle Arthur. It was easy to tell that this stringy man with features narrowed with suspicion was not an animal lover, not even of ones fattened up for slaughter. He jabbed his thumb at a space between a mud spattered Landrover and rusty ploughshare. With extreme trepidation for his E Type's paintwork, Walton managed to ease it into the gap without damaging anything. The girls slid out easily enough but Walton had to move over to the opposite side to avoid impaling the door on the ploughshare.

"That the nosy bleeder then?" Arthur growled.

"That's right, Nucky. You will be nice to him won't you?" said Poppy.

By the grunted reply Walton was unable to tell whether Arthur agreed or not.

"Coffee in kitchen," he announced as Walton joined them. "No milk. Bleeder never delivers on Sundays." Then he turned and walked back inside before the astronomer could introduce himself.

The bungalow was as ramshackle inside as it was out and twice as brown, like a panelled rabbit warren. It looked clean enough in the frugal light percolating through the half drawn curtains, but the visitors apparently weren't grand enough to be invited into the front room with its umbrella plant and lace antimacassars. They were ushered through a hall of Victorian prints and faded marble lino into the kitchen.

"It comes out of lake," Arthur grudgingly volunteered after he was satisfied the others had been sufficiently subdued by coffee corrosive enough to descale a kettle. "Circles a bit, then goes back."

Walton had to double take to realize he meant the UFO. "How often?" he asked.

"I don't have time to keep watch, and I never learned to count. Often enough."

"How large is it?"

"Large enough."

"Any military installations around here?"

"Not them bleeders. They've already had one farm off me. That's enough."

"On the other side of the hill ridge?"

"Only the lake."

"Shall I take you there?" asked Poppy.

"You gals stay here. I'll point the way out for him."

"Thanks." Walton sensed that the old man's intractability was provoked by more than congenital tetchiness.

"Oh, Nucky!" groaned Poppy.

"We can run if anything happens," added Bryony.

"Them as wants the glory can take the risks, and I've got a couple of curtains you can help me hang. Me fingers're rheumatic again. I'll take the gun out and look for him if he don't come back in a couple of hours." Arthur scooped up the mugs and threw the remaining dregs into the grate where he had been burning some rotten sacks.

The smoky stench that sizzled from them made Walton relieved to step outside before he could discover what colour the curtains were.

The range of hills, which prevented Arthur's monotonous fields sprawling even further, were strangely bland, as though a superhuman mason had flattened out their features. Walton stood stock still for a few seconds. He had an irrational suspicion that they were expecting his arrival.

Arthur turned back wearing a well-do-you-want-to-come-or-don't-you scowl. Putting his uneasy sensation down to overwork and too much red wine, Walton followed the farmer up a natural path worn into the granite of the hillside. When they reached the top, the lake on the other side of the hills stretched below them like a deep grey puddle of decomposing fish broth.

"Mostly sheer drop, but stroll along a bit and you'll find the way down to a stretch of shore."

"Thanks," said Walton. "The girls said they weren't in a hurry to get back, so I might be a couple of hours."

"Be back by three o'clock."

Before Walton could protest that he was a big boy now,

Arthur had turned and was walking back down to the bungalow.

As the astronomer descended to the wide lake he discovered that the water was even murkier than he expected. Anything attempting to survive in it would have needed the constitution of a Polaris submarine. The evil grey bubbles breaking its surface were certainly not filled with oxygen.

Walton cautiously made his way to the shoreline. After several near tumbles, he discovered a sizeable flat area gently lapped by the murky ripples. The hills on this side were quite craggy, as though the geological forces couldn't make up their mind whether they were icing a cake or popping corn. There were crumbs everywhere; even the shore was composed of shattered granite.

Walton scrutinized the encircling hillside for any sign of potholes or crevices, but for all their unevenness the rocks seemed to have closed ranks.

He stumbled over a small heap of pebbles covering an undulation on the beach. It was strangely out of place. Then something beneath the pile crackled in anger. UFOs he might have been prepared for, but lake dwelling monsters he was not. Half expecting a reptilian tail to lash into the air, Walton backed to the cover of the hillside. The noise soon died down but then, behind him, something else started to move. It sounded like boulders grinding on one another. Fearfully he turned to look. The thunderous noise was coming from inside the hill, as if he had disturbed the Troll King. He felt sweat on his brow and his heart thudded. If there were such unlikely phantoms he would have much preferred to meet The Lady of the Lake. The grinding eventually rumbled to a halt as if some slice of the hill had been lowered, or raised, inside it.

Walton did not like to admit he was intimidated, but he would have been a fool to deny it. Arthur's brain was probably not as addled as his manners suggested. The astronomer took out a handkerchief and mopped his forehead while considering his escape. He looked at his watch and wondered how long it was to three o'clock. Several hours. Its holographic face seemed to be telling him to dash back up the hillside while he still had the chance, but the recalcitrant logic of the scientific mind is a formidable thing. Something extraordinary was about to happen and Walton would never have forgiven himself for turning his back on it, even if his sense of self-preservation would.

He did not have long to wait. The rock face started to move, its surface revealing a hairline crack.

What infernal trigger had he stumbled onto? The crack widened to a fissure and was filled with intense light. Momentarily transfixed by the sight, he was suddenly aware of something behind him, something huge – watching.

Prickling in terror, Walton slowly turned to face the entity. The monster must have risen from the lake, and it was certainly no lady. It might have been spherical but it was giving off too much illumination to tell. Before he could tell his shaking legs to run, something struck Walton with the sticky force of a ten-ton candyfloss. Glued to its invisible magnetism, he was drawn slowly upwards like a giant jigged squid. He just had time to wonder how Arthur's shotgun would deal with this spider, before falling into a deep, dreamless coma.

5

Akaylia secured the bandage that was supporting Rabette's sprained ankle. "There you go, a work of art."

"I suppose it will have to do. I can see to it properly when you have gone."

"Why the anxiety to get rid of me? I want to prove continental drift before I go back up, at the very least."

"Oh that's real enough. It causes no end of bother down here."

"Go on, basalt baby?"

"All our cities were originally built on this level." Akaylia estimated they were at least a mile down. "But the same tectonics that push the planet's crust carry them deeper and deeper, much faster than the plates on the surface move. The shells of the first cities were only several yards thick when they were up here but, as they descended, we had to add to them. Eventually some became half a mile thick."

"No problem collecting energy down there anyway."

"That was the main reason they had to be abandoned. There was too much of it. The underfloor refrigeration couldn't cope with the heat."

At the mention of heat Akaylia realised she was uncomfortably warm and took off her shawl. Though the air-conditioning was an improvement on the polluted atmosphere above, she was having trouble in adapting to it. With a practiced accuracy she tossed the garment over a pipe snaking above their heads.

"If you must look around you might as well leave your satchel here. You have nothing in it that can match our equipment."

"What equipment do you have, you sensuous seismologist?"

"Anything needed to plug a crevice or divert a magma flow."

Akaylia hummed in bemusement at the powers of the tiny mortal. No longer able to contain her curiosity she began to tour the alien display of magnetometers, seismographs, P and S wave monitors and other equipment that defied her experience. Rabette's burrow, though not aesthetically successful – it was furnished with the same taste that encouraged him to wear the tartan suit – was quite cosy considering the functional fittings. In the centre of the ceiling was the shaft they had descended, and hidden amongst the clutter on the far wall was an entrance. That intrigued Akaylia most of all.

"Why don't any of your cities collapse? No normal buttressing could hold apart the sort of pressures down here."

"An energy field. All to do with switching molecules to line up and then holding them still. Acts as a heat barrier as well. The Drune knows more about that than I do."

"Drune? What dreadful dichotomy of parts goes to make up a 'Drune'?"

"Oh I shouldn't have mentioned it but, as I never meet anyone else to talk to, it slipped out. Forget I said it and I'll show you round this complex."

"All right little bleached blossom."

For a moment he regarded her critically. "I'll have to call

up my larger capsule. Apart from having plenty of room inside it's much more buoyant than the smaller one. I wouldn't fancy driving you over an ancient ventilation shaft in that. Gravity can behave in very strange ways the nearer you get to the mantle."

"Don't you have any fat Atlantians?"

"Not many, but the right amount of ballast is very important."

"I'll be worth it though. Most of me is very talented."

Akaylia watched Rabette carefully as he tapped out a code on a panel to call up a capsule.

"Stand over there on the weighbridge, will you." He pointed to a raised grating near the entrance.

Akaylia obeyed and a dial above her head spun round several times, to tell the capsule of the load to expect. She used the indignity as an excuse to take a look out of the entrance.

"Don't step off the platform," warned Rabette. "I never did get round to mending that railing."

Peering over the platform, she noted that the hazard was a drop of a thousand feet. A natural fold in the planet's crust had been buttressed apart until a chasm three times its depth had been formed.

"It was engineered to relieve the stress on the living complex below," Rabette called out from the room.

"What about the stress you've caused by interrupting the fold?"

"It's been diverted out and up into the adjoining folds. That's what caused the volcano. The pressure melted the rock."

Akaylia looked up at the vast ceiling and, in the dim light, she saw it was supported by jacks spanning distances that would have given a swallow vertigo. On the far side of the expanse a mechanical entity glittered into life. A machine that size should have made a horrendous noise but that would have not only been unpleasant down there, but dangerous as well. At the front of the vehicle, teeth the size of a two-storey house yawned in anticipation as it whirred on its way to satiate its appetite somewhere in the crust.

"How do you buttress the tunnels as you excavate them?" she called.

"Oh we don't dig tunnels any more. Only that creature I haven't mentioned knows how to do that now," came the reply. So somewhere in the mobile Christmas tree was the Drune. "Can you see the capsule yet?"

Akaylia spotted a small shape cutting across the bows of the hungry mechanical giant. "I can see something on the far side. It seems to be coming this way."

The excavator faintly thrummed off into blackness.

"Oh good. I'll just put everything onto automatic. Don't step into it until it's right up to the dock."

Akaylia looked at the bottomless pit below and agreed it was good advice.

The capsule was shaped like a cocoa pod, wrinkles and all. In its transparent upper half were several seats and a complexity of equipment in the rear. The lower hull must have contained its engine and buoyancy tanks.

"How fast can these things travel?"

Rabette joined her. "Oh very." He unbolted the safety seal and lifted the doors to the front seats.

"What sort of gas is contained in the floats?"

"It's quite inert. No need to worry. The engines don't cause sparks neither. There isn't too much hazard from gas down here because of the shielding, though we obviously don't light fires or invite in any active volcanoes. We keep the atmosphere well oxygenated, but the whole complex has too many safety shutters and automatic sprinklers against the risk of a firestorm. Step in – *step in!*"

"Which side shall I sit on?"

"Both if you like."

Aware of the usual rowing boat's reaction to her sudden boarding Akaylia climbed very gingerly into the rear of the capsule where she was confronted by a console duplicating the controls in the front. She carefully tucked in her knees and sat back to avoid knocking anything. With much more agility, Rabette bounced into the driver's seat before her. Running a rapid check on the engines, then a quick check on his monitor and the equipment in the back of the capsule, he switched on the propellers. As they started to move Akaylia found it a very odd sensation. With no road, wind or waves offering resistance, the only thing indicating their movement was the distance growing between the capsule and the dock.

"Can I see the complex below?"

"You can if you want. There's no one living down there though."

"Why not?"

"We're nearly extinct."

This reply took her by surprise. "How come?"

"Same reason anyone becomes extinct I suppose. One's genes cannot compete with the fatigue of staying alive."

"Then why bother to keep this place intact?"

"About twenty of us still live down here."

"Twenty? And in a place this size? Seems odd no-one else has colonized it?"

"What creatures in their right minds would choose to live down here?"

"Well, that means you must be round the bend. You speak our language well enough to get by, so why not try living upstairs?"

Rabette laughed. "Just look at me! How many humans do you think would be prepared to accept us? You said so yourself."

"I've got used to you though."

"As much as I would like to live above ground, I'm afraid

the selfish unpredictability of your kind worries me too much."

"Worries the hell out of me at times as well."

Rabette spiralled the capsule down to the entrance of a tunnel at the bottom of the chasm. A dial on the console in front of Akaylia began to register a slight thinning of oxygen. As they entered another chamber she was sure they were heading into surface daylight. It was filled with a jungle of vigorous, fruiting vegetation. Running water cascaded into a central lake surrounded by several small, cultivated plots. The only thing missing was bird song, though a few fluttering insects did dance in the rays of an artificial sun.

"We bred the insects as pollinators," Rabette explained, "and the sun is radiating all the necessary wavelengths – barring ultra violet – and chemicals of the natural sun. This farm used to supply half a city at one time. Gone a bit wild now though. It's a shame there's no one to export to."

After circling the verdant under-landscape they entered an even deeper tunnel. Here was a city, dimly illuminated after the synthetic gardens. Used to urban landscapes growing upward, Akaylia found the level buildings incongruously flat. They looked as though they were crouching in anticipation of a thunderstorm.

"Our most modern architecture. A little dreary isn't it."

Akaylia said nothing, as she didn't like to admit it was nowhere nearly as bad as her local town's.

"The grander styles are further down. The further down you go, the grander they get."

"Can we go down there?"

"I can't travel too far from the control. I'm responsible for this sector."

Rabette steered the capsule over a city that had probably been constructed with the movement of the Earth in mind. With no weather down there, they scarcely needed to worry about hurricanes or tornadoes. Akaylia wondered what it would be like to live without the odd breeze or hailstorm. Things should grow leggy and limp, but the stems of the foliage above looked robust enough and there wasn't enough of Rabette to reach the top shelf in any supermarket.

A siren and light on the capsule console flashing a message at its driver suddenly shattered her silent musings.

"Oh no," cursed Rabette.

"What's up?"

"Another magma leak. The wretched volcano sitting over us has the unpleasant habit of erupting upside down."

"But that volcano's extinct."

"Not down here it isn't."

"Well what d'you know!"

"I'll have to plug it."

"But it could erupt upstairs then."

"That's what volcanoes are meant to do. We've enough trouble controlling the stresses down here without needing to worry about neurotic volcanoes which don't know which way to erupt."

"But your entrance tunnel leads through it."

"I'll get the Drune to make another one. As long as it never finds out about you it might agree to do it."

"When are you going to operate?"

"Now. Everything I need is on board and it won't wait."

"You're kidding! How?"

"Blow the magma outflow up and bring down its roof to divert the lava away from us."

"Where can I get out?"

"You can't. There isn't time. I thought you wanted to look around?"

"Not inside volcanoes. How will this capsule behave out of the shielded tunnels anyway?"

"I've pressurized the hull." Akaylia now realised that the wrinkles in the capsule, which she had thought were part of its supporting skeleton, had been ironed out from the inside. "It's not the pressure that's the danger up there, though."

"Surprise me?"

"We lose more operatives through having the heat shields buckle."

Akaylia didn't have time to be terrified. To her astonishment her weight suddenly doubled as the capsule accelerated like a bullet through a vacuum.

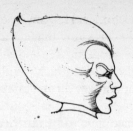

6

Several hours after his bizarre abduction, Walton woke to a monstrous hangover. Something told him that coming round was as good an idea as agreeing to introduce a gaggle of art students to scientific observation. Any one of them would have appreciated that experience far more. He wondered if he should go back to sleep, but his head throbbed. It much preferred to be upright, though the spherical room in which he found himself gave little indication in what direction "up" lay. There were no corners anywhere to take reference from, and every circular and oval fitting was built into the walls regardless of gravity.

Tentatively Walton placed one foot on what he thought to be the floor and held the sides of the couch for fear of hitting the ceiling. The air pressure seemed standard enough for safety and no magnetic force insisted he remain prone. Then he noticed a small circular cabinet by the couch and on it a tumbler half full of peach coloured liquid. He didn't need to read it to know it was saying "drink me", but his reflexes weren't up to facing any molecule-moulding experiences. Rubbing his temples, he attempted to revive the circulation to his brain but the logjam in his arterial tributaries wouldn't budge. He glowered suspiciously at the tumbler.

A creamy voice suddenly regaled him from nowhere. "My, my – you do have a thick skull. Most others stay unconscious for far longer. Never mind, Professor! If you can manage to lift it, drink the solution at your elbow. Your quicksilver faculties will return instantly, I promise you."

If the light tone of the voice had not been so smooth Walton would have been enraged by its casual sarcasm. Hoping its owner would be eventually susceptible to the same elementary psychology as Poppy, Walton stayed silent and swigged down the potion. As promised, his synapses started to make accurate contact and his wits returned. Reasonably sure he was upright; he rose and, without faltering, strode towards the only exit he could see.

"Oh don't disturb the Captain," the voice sighed. "The sight of humans scares him."

Walton stopped and looked up with an uncertain frown.

"Oh, I'm probably more like you than him – but then, I'm not really like anyone."

The astronomer scowled.

"Oh well, if you must satisfy your curiosity. You've already complicated everything so much that a few more knots might make a nice piece of macramé to hang us both with. Go ahead. Further bedevil my existence."

Only hesitating to wonder why the communicative creature should have had an "existence" instead of life, Walton pushed what he assumed to be the door control.

"Goodbye for now," the voice sang after him. "Try not to frighten the aliens won't you."

Walton suspected that this was some cosmic practical joke engineered by delinquent advanced life forms. Bored with being so intelligent they had decided to break the monotony by sneaking up on more lowly humans to play infantile tricks, but the craft in which he found himself did not appear to be large enough for interstellar travel. As it was shaped like a globe it had probably been designed to negotiate the turbulence of planetary atmospheres.

Appraising the spherical walls with a cool judgement, Walton reminded himself that there was nothing like terror to increase the size of a monster. This craft was nowhere near as large as the beast that had carried him off.

He stopped at the padded junction of three passages. There were no hard surfaces to produce echoes and it was so claustrophobic he wanted to punch a hole in a wall to find fresh air. Instead he saw what he assumed to be the entrance to the craft's control room. Wearing his most annoyed expression he strode onto the balcony inside. At his appearance there was the sudden clacking of alien tongues from a couple of highly agitated and extraordinary creatures. They were too animated to be totally reptilian, but they certainly weren't mammalian or marsupial. They also had little colour sense; it was difficult to tell where their skins ended and preposterous clothes began. They looked like the demons Inigo Jones might have designed for a masque. All they lacked were the horns and forks, and the clumsy ruffs were straight out of a Handelian opera, whether anatomically theirs' or not. If there was anything worse than a grotesque alien, it was a silly grotesque alien.

Now be reasonable, Walton told himself. They might be repulsive to look at and possess no scruples about abducting unsuspecting humans, but that was no reason why his intellect should be reduced to the bigotry he despised in others. The alien crew seemed less open-minded about him. In a flurry of fearful annoyance the smaller of the two snapped on a switch and gushed its irritated tones into a grid above it.

"Oh dear," the original creamy voice sighed back in resignation. "You have upset our hairless little friends haven't you."

Though aware of his considerable size, Walton had never regarded himself as unattractive, let alone repellent enough to scare a couple of aliens. He folded his arms to indicate he intended to stay where he was.

"I suppose that means I must come and fetch?" The voice seemed resigned. Walton glowered at the grid. "For someone with the intellect to be curious you say precious little?" Still there was no reply from the scientist. "If you would like to step outside I will meet you there. I won't come in. The sight of me upsets them even morc. Oh, by the way, I'm a Drune."

Not seeing how he could avoid it, Walton reluctantly complied, hardly sorry to be out of that alien clicking noise.

In the outer passage, he waited long enough between the claustrophobic walls to grow irritated.

Soon a bizarre figure dropped from nowhere and casually strode forward to meet him. Clad in dense black like a velvet shadow there was no pretence of the normal, living human about it; the contours would never have accommodated any human genitalia or even a pouch. Although humanoid, the astronomer guessed that it was a very sophisticated android.

The Drune's shoulders were wide and powerful. The hips were also flared but the waist was very narrow and wasp like, making it impossible to tell what gender its designer had intended to model it on. An amazing upward sweeping ruff of shimmering silver hair concealed its head, neck and parts of its cheeks. Despite the male hairline of its sideburns, the centre of its face was visible. It was oddly feline and finely sculptured. However, the metallic grey tinge of the skin and complementary tinsel gleam of the hair lent the features a cool severity, as though they were mantled in frost. It made no effort to mellow its satanic appearance; this was more like the real demon.

Yet the Drune spoke Walton's language, and no doubt thirty others as well, with such assurance and lucidity it was difficult to believe this derived from anything mechanical.

"Welcome to our little burrow, Professor," it purred.

"Doctor," Walton corrected.

"So you do speak," it gasped mockingly. "I was afraid you might."

"What the devil is this place?"

"How about the gateway to Hell." Walton scowled, provoking a shrug from the Drune, who continued, "Or perhaps you're only dreaming. But then, I can see you, so perhaps it is I who am suffering the nightmare."

"Robots cannot dream."

"Not even of electric sheep?"

"Or read science fiction."

"Then I must be a figment of your imagination."

"I still want to know where I am?"

"Mustn't grind your teeth, it cracks the enamel."

Walton was tempted to ask how it knew he still had his own teeth, but didn't want to give the Drune any more excuse for sarcasm. Unfortunately, it must have had a telepathy chip.

"Dentists charge so much nowadays."

"So what else do you know about me?"

"The official CV, or just the hang-ups?"

"You don't really know anything, do you? It's just an act. You're guessing like a stage fake."

This was the Drune's cue. Its purple eyes lit up as though it was its birthday and it gleefully pounced on those insecurities Walton Clarke had so far successfully kept from a prying world. "I know all the wonders your mighty intellect contains."

"So what are they, Drune?"

"The comfort of logic for an absurdly speculative science perhaps? Pictures of the planets in computer enhanced colours and maps of this Universe in red shifted illusion?"

"So what does shape the Universe, Drune?"

"Gravity." The Drune raised its hands in a maniacal gesture. "How is it an astronomer your weight had not yet found a way to measure gravitons? But then, you've already failed in so many directions."

Walton wasn't a violent fellow. The worst he had ever done was pick a student up by the seat of his pants and one ear, or kick the boot of his old car when it was unable to clamber out of the shallowest of ruts. But now his fingers twitched as he contemplated murder.

"How do you know so much about me?" he growled.

"Oh, I know everything."

Reluctantly Walton believed it. Discomfort tempered his inclination to dismantle the machine. He preferred his puppets with strings, safely miming to a ventriloquist's voice. Even if the Drune had been benevolent, the thought would not have consoled him. The memory required to activate the creature must have taken years to programme, and the scorn with which it used its knowledge could only have come from the Devil.

"I'm so sorry you had to stumble on us like that – but you were hunting UFOs weren't you?"

"How did you –" Walton stopped as it raised its black gloved hands in mock apology. "Oh yes, you know everything, don't you."

"Why so resentful, Doctor? Logic suggests that at least one other creature in the Universe must know more than you."

Now the Drune sounded like a senior lecturer who was treating Walton like an unreliable office gofer.

"What do you mean by that?"

"Oh don't be upset. I'm not blaming you for wanting to educate the less intellectual into deserting their comforting fantasies about the likes of us, but . . ."

"But what?"

"But you cannot distil the knowledge of the Universe in a teapot and expect to pour everyone a cup from it. Even a teapot the size of your ego isn't that large."

Damn this infernal Drune. Before it could take a grand tour of his marital problems as well, Walton demanded, "Why did you bring me down here?"

"I didn't. The Captain panicked. He's always panicking. The odd sightings by a human of our test flights had never created a problem before because it's not the sort of thing sensible people believe in, is it? But he thought you were a little too close. And with those big feet how could you fail to tread on the trigger to the entrance for the main bays."

"So this is only a scout craft then?"

The Drune raised a finger to its mischievous mouth. "Not so loud please. Come with me. We will have to think of some way to get you back."

"What if I don't want to co-operate?"

"Have you ever tried to strangle an android?"

This one was so sophisticated its self-defence system must have been correspondingly effective. Walton's fingers ceased to twitch with murderous intent, realising the massive jolt of voltage they might have received in the attempt.

He followed the Drune into a corridor, which led under the lake from the spacecraft to a larger complex. This chamber seemed to be some sort of junction where passages radiated up, down and out in all directions. The Drune led him straight on, into the most illuminated.

"What were those creatures back there?"

The Drune's casual manner was too controlled to give anything away. "Oh, you'd call them aliens. I call them a nuisance. Totally incapable of learning to speak a human tongue."

"They could hardly have the right vocal cords."

"There is one that has. And if you're very lucky you may not have to meet her."

Walton needed to believe that the Drune was genuinely trying to help him, but the aura of the creature was of mischievous malice.

"Not very friendly, is she?"

"I've never been able to tell. Now please put your feet down very quietly and try not to walk into anything. I'm going to dim the lights as we go."

"I'll take your arm then."

The Drune recoiled. "No! Whatever you do, don't touch me!"

"All right." Walton assumed there was a force field of some sort surrounding the android. "Just don't direct me near any holes."

"And keep quiet."

"This is some sort of joke, isn't it?"

The Drune didn't seem too bothered with what Walton believed. It gave the impression of a parent dealing with someone else's rather tiresome infant. "No. That snivelling Captain of hers blames me for every mistake he makes. And you happen to be the superlative to date. The real joke will be your trying to convince anyone you were kidnapped by a UFO."

Walton was bursting to answer but, just as the Drune dimmed the tunnel lights, the air suddenly cracked with a hair-raising sound; an alien talking a human dialect with its thin forked tongue.

"Drune," it whirred. "Come to me."

"All right," the Drune replied, furtively directing Walton to hide in the shadows of another junction.

But it was too late.

"And bring your human friend with you."

7

As the capsule left the second pressure lock, Akaylia was at last restored to her usually sufficient weight. Outside, the irregular walls writhed with heat and the atmosphere shimmered like the inside of a kiln, only this kiln could glaze steel onto furnace bricks. From a safe distance Akaylia would have been curious about the composition of the glowing rock, but her thoughts had turned to fire prevention. She should have asked Rabette whether this expedition was really safe but was afraid of an honest answer. The little man seemed more irritated by the tedious behaviour of the artificial volcano than awed by the prospect of it dropping its magma chamber on them at any moment.

Their route continued through the acridly glaring tunnels carved by rivers of boiling rock. Akaylia's mouth was dry and her appetite had contracted to nothing for the first time since she was introduced to jellied eels. Rabette was driving them straight towards the volcano's magma chamber. If his ancestors had possessed the same contempt for the raw powers of nature it was hardly surprising they were almost extinct.

"Hadn't we better apply the brake now, you snippet of super being?" she asked tentatively.

"Oh no," came the breezy reply. "The faster we move the safer we are. Pass over the explosive pod I primed will you."

Akaylia silently obeyed.

"And the suit at the very back."

Puzzled, she lunged awkwardly over the other equipment to reach it. The suit was light, white and made with many layers of fabric resembling asbestos, but felt like woven metal. All its pieces were welded together in ridges like massive French seams, and the helmet had several locks as well as a screw deeper than that on any coffee jar Akaylia had ever wrestled open. There was an odd sloshing sound as she pushed it over to Rabette; the suit's cooling system was liquid based. Then she realized why he wanted it.

"You're not going out there!"

"It's all right. There's a pressure lock in the roof. You'll be quite safe."

"You are totally deranged. Why can't you just chuck the explosive out?"

"Because if it isn't wedged into something stable the magma will incinerate it before it can detonate. It must be time-set so we have the chance to get out of here."

"There must be some rational argument against your logic." Rabette started to pull on the cumbersome suit. "Why don't we just sit here and discuss this in a calm and meaningful way?"

Rabette had obviously never needed counselling for confusion. It had never occurred to him to avoid the inevitable by having an emotional crisis. By the time he was kitted out, they had reached the magma chamber.

As the molten furnace boiled below them the atmosphere batted the capsule from side to side. Rabette merely increased its speed causing Akaylia's stomach to hit the back of her seat. She imagined she could smell frying but dare not look to see where it came from. By no stretch of the imagination could she picture inoffensive pumice being made from that soup of radiant orange malice.

Rabette busily punched up on his monitor pictures of map after map of crustal fractures, until he eventually seemed satisfied.

"I'll let it blow its top down there," he decided. "That will take it right back down to the mantle and a natural volcano's roots where it'll be able to release its pressure."

Rabette guided the capsule from the magma chamber into an outflow the other side.

"How about explaining the controls in case I have to rescue you?"

"Don't touch anything on your dashboard unless it's to drive yourself out of here if I can't make it back. You should know how to do that by now."

"I was thinking about scooping you up if necessary."

"You wouldn't get the chance. The explosive pod has to have a short timing. There will only be a matter of minutes to escape."

"Have it your own way you loony leporid."

Rabette selected a spot high in the tunnel of the main outflow. There was a narrow ridge and handy crevice above it.

"Now remember what I said," he told Akaylia like a primary school teacher. Then he lowered a heavy clear shutter between himself and her seat.

Rabette checked that his suit was hermetically sealed and his atmosphere pressurized. Thinking of how the planet would suffer if real rabbits ever learnt to excavate on this scale, Akaylia sat back and stared as the lid of his segment slid down. "Why worry?" she thought. "He's so dotty he must know what he's doing." Who was she, a mere mortal geologist and failed potholer, to presume to tell an expert how to proceed? Comforted with such thoughts of humility so alien to her ego, she watched Rabette step from the capsule and onto the shuddering ledge. Despite the efforts to reassure herself, she memorized the functions of the buttons on the passenger dashboard.

Rabette seemed to be doing quite well. His movements were awkward because of the bulk of the suit but, despite the boiling furnace below him, he wedged the explosive into the small crevice. Carefully he started the timer.

But he was too eager to get back into the capsule. As he turned, the narrow ledge crumpled beneath him. Before he could grasp the capsule he slid down the smooth wall towards the magma. Not even the wonder suit would prevent him from being incinerated when he reached it. In desperation his foot found a near invisible crack in the wall. Unfortunately it was his sprained foot and Akaylia could see it was not going to take his weight for long. Frantically he waved her away.

Akaylia had worked out enough to drive the capsule. She floated it level with Rabette and angled it against the wall to scrape him up. He had no choice but to tumble into his seat. Only hesitating to close the capsule roof, Akaylia reversed the vehicle's programme so it went darting back along its route. Aware the tunnel would cease to exist at any moment, she never bothered to open the partition to see if Rabette was still alive.

Almost across the central chamber, an almighty explosion rocked the capsule. The magma flared angrily as part of the roof fell into it. The blazing orange blancmange lashed up the side of the chamber in an attempt to push through the alternative fracture Rabette had selected, but the gap was still not wide enough and the chamber started to fill. They had to make it to the escape tunnel before that was blocked as well.

Skimming the murderous maelstrom, Akaylia struggled to avoid colliding with the ceiling. She felt muscles she had never used before tensing under the strain. At last she managed to bumble the fatigued capsule into the access tunnel and to the safety of the pressure lock. The craft's propellers were practically jammed, sealed together by the heat, and its power exhausted.

Once on the other side of the atmosphere locks Akaylia lowered the shutter between her and Rabette. She pulled him out of the suit, expecting to find nicely broiled chicken. He was badly shocked and heat fatigued, but she was thankful not to discover a worse mess.

With some bullying and pleading Akaylia brought Rabette round briefly enough to tap the co-ordinates of a medical station into the capsule dashboard. She didn't have the heart to tell him before he passed out again that their transport was unable to go anywhere. She climbed out onto the narrow landing bay and, using the control on the wall, called up another capsule.

When the vehicle arrived, Akaylia lifted Rabette into it, then, taking the pilot's seat, fed in the instructions to the medical station. The capsule darted on its way, angling corners and ascending and descending tunnels with robotic precision.

"I could learn to enjoy driving one of these things," Akaylia mused to herself.

Before the idea could trigger her normally anarchic impulses, they arrived. Gathering up the semiconscious bundle, she carried him into the medical station. As soon as they entered the station, everything sprang into life about them: lights, air-conditioning, swivelling couch. As Rabette and his companions were not in immediate reach of each other the medication had to be automatic. All she need do was place him on the couch.

Rabette was presented before an array of diagnosing scanners. When satisfied, the panels above radiated their cure. Akaylia was perversely pleased that the patient did not leap up right away in the peak of health. There was a proper and gratifying period of complaints and moaning before he opened his eyes.

"How's the jugged hare, then?" she asked.

Suddenly realizing where he was and who was inspecting him, Rabette snapped feebly, "I told you to clear off. Why didn't you listen?"

"I'm a slow learner."

He was too befuddled to question how she had managed to save him.

"Would you rather be left alone for a while?"

"Yes," he agreed.

"Can I borrow the capsule?"

"All right, but don't try and take it out of this sector. And stay away from the Drune."

"But of course, fretsome fellow. What would I want with a 'Drune'?"

"They don't make very good soup." Rabette's eyes became glazed again.

"They what?"

"Too much hair . . ." So saying, he rapidly drifted off to sleep.

Soup was the last thing on Akaylia's mind. Even solid food had to take its place in the back burner of her thoughts as opportunism elbowed appetite aside. She threw a light blanket over Rabette then bounced out to the capsule.

Discovering the way back to the chasm below Rabette's control chamber, Akaylia spiralled the capsule down to the tunnel where she had seen the excavating machine disappear. The light in there had an ominous hue to it, but she pushed on all the same.

The passages and junctions were less ancient and some of them had been recently renovated. She must have been at the boundary of the sector Rabette had warned her not to go beyond. That suspicion was confirmed as the capsule slowly murmured to a halt. Akaylia was not going to be so easily put off. She climbed out and started to walk.

8

No longer bothering to dim the lights, the Drune led Walton through a maze of passages deep into the range of hills. The astronomer might have tried to escape but he knew he would never find his way out and was curious to know where he was being taken. Was it possible to encounter even stranger things than those he had already confronted?

The Drune was suddenly uncommunicative. Realizing its mistress was watching, its playful platitudes had waned into robotic implacability. Walton thought this was a pity in a way. He hated it for treating him like an incontinent yak, yet he half wanted it to convince him that all true geniuses were mechanical monsters.

At the junction of several tunnels they came to a lift shaft.

"How deep are we going?" Walton demanded before agreeing to step into one of the cages.

"Very deep", the Drune refused to console him. "Don't make a fuss. It's quite safe. I overhauled the system myself."

Walton glared dubiously at its black gloves. "What? With your own fair hands? What is wrong with your hands, anyway? Was it an accident?"

"Don't be absurd. I'm an android."

It was a silly question, but the vehemence with which it protested its mechanized nature made Walton all the more curious. However, the speed with which they descended glued his tongue to the roof of his mouth.

Because they were falling like a stone in a vacuum, it was not possible to register much, though Walton spotted large, half-lit underground cities as many and as varied as any on the planet's surface. Some considerable way down was a great chamber with gargantuan structures decorated with pretentious statuary. He assumed they had something to do with rulers and government; those ornate ribbed and vaulted roofs were hardly to keep the rain off.

The Drune noted his interest in the city. "Chipperti", it said with no hint as to whether that was the name of the place or the droppings of some albino bat.

As the lift slowed, Walton was convinced he had fallen through into another world. They were soaring over a vaulted chamber that housed a city more eerie and strange than anything else he had so far seen. Here and there it flickered with light, but was quite deserted.

"Rosipolees. Not built by us. The inhabitants left it centuries ago but we make use of its generators," explained the Drune, disclaiming any of the other questions Walton was exploding to ask. "Just a warning – you may take it or leave it as you please – but don't decide to get stroppy with Pyg. After you've set eyes on her you probably won't feel inclined to."

If the words didn't actually dampen Walton's huge confidence, they certainly blew cool air over it. The lift descended through the floor of the city and brought them to a smaller complex underneath. Walton cautiously left the cage and followed the Drune. This world was more recent than the one above. It was newly excavated and, considering they were several miles down, the circulating air was as fresh as a crisp spring day. The passages were wide and angular and wore a just-painted look.

Finally they came to a shutter, which opened instantly. The Drune beckoned Walton inside. He would rather have explored the city above, but reluctantly stepped into the chamber.

In the dim lighting he saw an indistinct figure seated on a dais above them. He didn't care much for the silhouette it presented and the hackles on the back of his neck rose in anticipation of being able to see it clearly. Then he noticed something even more disconcerting. It not only had the effrontery to speak a human language, but also breathed Earth's air without the rapid panting of the aliens above. Against the tocsins alerting his better instincts and the warnings of the Drune, the shock made Walton blurt out a recrimination about aliens corrupting Earth's atmosphere. The words may have been tangled but it did not need a linguist to unravel their offensiveness.

There was a menacing silence during which Walton fancied he could hear the Drune's circuits crackle in apprehension.

"Aliens?" whirred a voice that lingered in the large chamber like electrified mist. "You are the aliens. This is our planet."

The figure was suddenly illuminated. Walton froze at what confronted him. Though the same species as the two males above, Pyg was twice their size and a thousand times more fearsome. Her hairless, scale-less skin resembled mother-of-pearl. It coruscated with the pulses of arteries and veins circulating blood. There was no nose and gills at the side of the head. Nor was there a visible mouth and the voice came from the gills. This made the louring oblong eyes all the more intimidating. On a face bald of all other features they were like animated beacons waiting to spotlight prey. Her body was clothed in a lacy garment that rippled with a movement of its own. Walton could see that, although bipedal, Pyg had none of the mammary equipment of a human.

Being so explicitly confronted by this female, the astronomer was filled with more affection for his wives than he had ever entertained before. Here was a species where the male laid table and his mate laid down the law. Even the asexual Drune showed signs of trepidation.

"Come here, human," Pyg told him. Walton obeyed. "So the Drune has let you into our little secret, has it?"

"Little?"

"Don't you appreciate figures of your own speech from aliens? What is your name?"

"Walton Clarke."

Pyg beckoned to the Drune. It approached casually, though Walton saw it was tense in every limb. It all seemed to be part of a game they played. Although the alien was the one in control, the Drune's strange dignity did not flinch. Walton hated himself for admiring the majestic machine.

"Have you rectified the transmission imbalance yet?"

"Yes. Everything is stable. The Ossiane engineers still think their sole purpose in life is to put out volcanoes before they can fall on you."

"They haven't discovered . . . ?"

The Drune laughed. "Goodness no, they'll never find out you're down here."

"Then, be silent, fool."

"Oh, I wouldn't worry about the human. He is utterly lacking in imagination. He just blundered into the place like a Boy Scout without a compass."

"Why didn't you report his presence to me?"

"I didn't want to bother you. I was going to give him an amnesia drug then return him like the others."

Pyg's voice clicked calculatingly. "Now he's heard so much why don't we let this one know everything?"

This seemed to startle the Drune, as though she had merely proposed the idea to throw it off balance. "He probably won't be interested."

Any subtleties of the interactions were lost on Walton. "Of course I'm interested."

"He really isn't very bright. I'm sure you could find a better subject."

"I want this one," insisted Pyg. "It's not often I have the opportunity to converse with a human. The experiment will be interesting. You can do what is necessary afterwards."

Walton was too curious to worry about what "necessary" meant. "Why do you insist this is your planet?"

Pyg loured at such brazenness from an inferior creature, one that thought its kind had inherited the Earth with no strings attached. "I am descended from the first intelligent species that evolved on this planet. As you are related to mammals, we are descended from what you insultingly refer to as dinosaurs. Only we were never reptiles and never cold blooded. Your generic chauvinism dismissed the truth of our evolution with images of monstrous carnivores and brainless herbivores. But we were more diverse than you, and survived longer."

"Then why did you become extinct?"

"We did not become extinct. We left the planet because it had grown too small for us. We used it as a museum and experimental base until . . ."

"The Cretaceous comet," deduced Walton.

"The resulting pollution from its impact wiped out most of the wildlife in our zoo. However, some organisms did survive."

"Organisms?"

"The experimental creatures we created. They developed into mammals. We engineered them so they would have a chance of survival."

"That's preposterous!"

"Preposterous but true, human. You are nothing more than the product of one of our experiments. We designed you. You need not look so incredulous. I'm sure the only thing that prevents your species from doing the same thing is its backwardness."

"Even if it could be true, what are you doing here now?"

"Just completing a small experiment."

"Experiment?"

"To see how the progeny we invented are coping with their evolution."

"You mean you're still monitoring us as part of your experiment?"

"Sluggish creatures such as you supply little data of interest. We sometimes intervene to liven things up: positive ion poisoning, blocking certain pleasure centres, *et cetera*. With the prime human motives for living being sex and self, this should add considerable interest to our observations."

"But that's inhuman."

"Am I not a dinosaur?"

"What about compassion?"

"As an experimental subject, you hardly merit compassion. Though I would not begrudge you the compassion you show for the other animals on this planet. I believe you show your experimental animals compassion by destroying them painlessly when they are beyond further use. We shall offer you a similar sympathy."

"But that is monstrous. Haven't you any idea of what you're implying?"

"Of course we have. For millennia we have been fascinated by the manner in which species evolve intelligence. It's an attractive bonus that it was happening right here on our home planet when we last decided to survey it."

"But you left this world. You can no longer have any claim on it."

"We can claim the intellectual authority to do whatever we have the power to. Would you hold such a conversation with a monkey whose brain you are about to dissect?"

"But . . ." Walton's words foundered.

"Such pleas for tolerant niceties only apply when they derive from parity of intellect. Yours species has followed this self evident truth against the rest of the planet's population ever since you lost your tails and grew wisdom teeth. Surely it should come as no great surprise that a superior life form now assumes that same prerogative."

"You won't get away with it." Walton would have launched a murderous attack on Pyg, but his strength was suddenly sapped.

Pyg looked at the monitor beside her in disappointment. "You can take him away now."

The Drune shrugged. "I told you he wasn't worth it."

"Make sure his memory is totally erased. No half measures. When he's returned to his species he must never be able to communicate with another person again."

"Easier to kill him."

"Do as I tell you."

Walton listened with horror to the conversation. His limbs then obeyed the Drune's command to follow it back to the lift.

"Now look what your big mouth has done," the Drune told its speechless victim. "I warned you didn't I? A couple of blackout shots, and whoosh – not a twinge, apart from a two-hour hole in your life. But this – painful! I'm the humane sort myself. I prefer to put the patient down, but you heard what the lady said."

They alighted from the lift half way up the shaft to enter the Drune's laboratory, a chamber filled with equipment unrecognizable to Walton.

He felt his iron will melting away under the Drune's casually cruel and one-sided conversation. "Just sit over there." Walton's body obeyed. "If it helps, I do know you would like to break me into little pieces. So I'll try and make it quick. I'm afraid there's no anaesthetic for this procedure but after I've finished you won't remember the pain. In fact, you won't remember anything."

9

Not long afterwards, the secret entrance Walton had discovered in the hillside opened wide. A pod-like craft slipped out and glided up to the other side of the hill, then silently returned.

Pyg's minion went to its laboratory and idly pushed keys until its records picked out, "Astronomer, Clarke – Walton . . ." It was hardly reassuring, rifling through the past life of the person it had just been ordered to destroy. The Drune switched the control to another chamber, so deep it floated on the moho. Then it programmed its capsule to take it down.

At that level the pressure and heat were perilously intense, but the complex was protected by molecularly rigid shields so thick the motion of the liquid rock below was no more hazardous than the ripples made by a dragonfly on a calm pond.

After passing through the last pressure lock, the Drune disembarked and entered a dimly lit chamber.

Cloaked in comforting blackness it sank onto a couch. In cold concentration its purple eyes gazed at a globe pulsating with light. The large sphere's skin shimmered with a mix of rare gases and impulses waiting to be called into life, but this egg had not been designed to hatch. There were probably creatures throughout the Galaxy capable of laying shells every bit as large and spherical, but none of them could have hatched the fantasies born from the Drune's creation. In the hands of psychiatrists it could have conjured up enough nightmares in their patients' minds to drive them even madder. The Drune's brain was too finely tuned to take that sudden plunge, though. Mad it might eventually become, but gradually and for different reasons.

One sliver of thought, one unguarded impulse, could activate the globe. Should it? Most things the Drune understood, but this hellish creation had evolved beyond its own comprehension. Pyg would probably destroy both egg and her minion if she learnt about it. When activated, the turmoil it engendered in the Drune's own mind was hardly worth the risk. But it was like a narcotic; no longer a release, but a necessity.

How many demons was the Drune strong enough to call up today? How may skeins of fantasy could it absorb, in order to shield out ugly reality before Pyg compelled it to another odious task? The Drune was not only Pyg's eyes and ears in the labyrinth, but the solver of any problems threatening the complex, whether geological or mortal. Swatting annoying humans or dousing volcanic activity were not things the Drune had been programmed for. But the less Pyg understood of its true origins the better. The truth would have shaken even her cold composure.

As the Drune raised its hands and briefly concentrated, the large globe pulsated into life, voracious for the mental images to fill it. The Drune fed it its reflection. A pair of glistening eyes stared back mockingly, the corners of its mouth crinkled with cynicism. The Drune's crimes were reflected in those features.

Who was this lady with the bright magenta eyes? A

parent beckoning, as if mistaking it for a lost child. What should it say to her? Then her real offspring came into view. It was a tiny creature, holding a gossamer glider six times its size. With a flick of its tiny wrist the glider was launched into the updraught from the ventilation system. What a remarkable package of biology this child was destined to become, unstintingly passing on its genius; dividing impossible equations and multiplying them into solutions.

But they were asking too much and gave nothing in return. They vaunted it on a pedestal too high to climb down from, yet denied it entry to the Hall of Sensation. It could solve the problems of the empire but not walk from the cage of its own biology. The Drune ached to show it how to become a machine, even a flawed one with addictive fantasies of its own. It tried to push the illusion from the screen, but it would not budge.

Were they still sitting in eternal judgment? What crime had this expressionless mortal presaged to deserve total banishment? They said it was unclean because nature had denied it gender. So they placed it in a cocoon where it would never be found. Abruptly the Drune managed to extricate its thoughts.

The grey smoke from a blue dragon pushed the images back. Its friendly jaws devoured the smoke and left an abyss of crisp, welcoming blackness. The Drune liked the dragon. It called up another, purple, like its eyes. Then a cat, pompously plump and brownish ginger. It smiled. The cat fluttered its huge eyelashes in a strangely coy way.

"What are you doing down here?" asked the Drune.

"Why shouldn't I be, Silver Hair? Every home needs a cat."

"Only human ones; they encourage rats."

"Then every Drune deserves a tiger."

The Drune laughed. "Is that what you are – a tiger?"

"Oh yes, and burning bright, in the shadows of the night." Then it faded, leaving its smile till last.

The Drune felt mildly reassured. Perhaps it was not mad after all. Perhaps the fact that it could hold conversations with its own fantasies and not think it unnatural meant that it was too mad to realize otherwise.

Images of landscapes, quilts of quasars and creating clouds swirled through the crystal globe drowning the feline illusion. Inexorably, the craving that had given rise to the stabbing thoughts faded. Starved of the Drune's hallucinations the screen became still.

10

Walton had no idea how long he had been lying on the ground. Were it not for the hard nudge of Uncle Arthur's boot to test whether he was still alive or not, he would probably have slept on.

"I must have blacked out." Walton groaned. "I feel as though I've been here ages."

"No chance. I searched this bit two hours ago. I reckon you toppled down that hill shortly after I went by."

"Oh my head! What time is it?"

"About six." Arthur tucked the shotgun under his arm and pulled him up.

Poppy and Bryony saw them and dashed over to help.

"What happened? Where have you been? Are you hurt?"

But Walton couldn't remember enough to answer any of them as they took him back to the bungalow.

"You can't drive home in that state," Arthur declared. "The girls'll have to do it."

Walton was in no condition to argue with that. His head now throbbed so hard he couldn't even say what colour his car was, let alone find the ignition.

"Did you see anything though?" Poppy insisted for the umpteenth time.

After the third cup of Arthur's coffee and whisky, Walton managed to answer, "Not a thing. That's the odd part. I must have been doing something."

"Perhaps you were picked up by a flying saucer?" Bryony suggested hopefully.

In the process of sneering away the suggestion, Walton was set to thinking. As he couldn't remember what had happened, how could he be sure? All the nerve-jangling way back to his home the possibility irritated him like an implacable itch. To compound the confusion, he was helped to his front door and greeted by all the members of his previous marriages. Flying saucers were not the only thing he should have remembered something about.

"My goodness," declared Helen, his poodle breeding second wife. "What have you ladies been giving him to drink?"

"Uncle Arthur's whisky," Poppy answered with such innocence she had to believe her.

Janice had no suspicions though. "Oh darling, what happened to you?" She took her husband from the young women and hauled him inside.

Helen, Lettice and Ethel looked at each other with "she'll-learn-soon-enough" expressions.

"Won't you two ladies come in as well?" Helen told them. "Let us know what happened to the big booby and give us all a laugh."

Bryony and Poppy looked apprehensively at each other but as no one offered to take the ignition keys from them they had no choice.

Walton was pushed down onto the settee. The art students perched on stools a safe distance away trying to look as inconspicuous as possible. With avid interest, the older women watched how Janice attempted to bring her husband round to some sort of sensibility. Failing in that, she persuaded Poppy and Bryony to tell all they knew.

"Well goodness," chuckled Ethel when they had finished. "Perhaps he did get to meet a space ship after all."

"Pity we'll never know who came off worst."

"Please, Helen," protested Janice. "The poor man is in a very bad way."

Poppy coughed politely. "I . . . I think we'd better go now."

"No chance," ordered Helen. "I'll take you home in my car. It's asking for trouble walking about after dark."

Neither of them dared to argue. A cold dinner was preferable.

"I'll bring him round." Lettice produced some smelling salts.

Walton gasped back to sensibility. "What are you all here for? I don't owe any alimony."

"Charming," observed Helen, then told Janice. "I don't suppose he remembers your birthday either?"

"What are you talking about?" he demanded.

"It's your birthday, darling," Janice reminded him. "The girls brought the children round for a party. But you never showed up."

"Oh Christ!"

Helen gave a hard laugh. "Oh don't worry about it. They didn't notice. They're probably too tired to bother after breaking your home up."

"Where are they now?"

"Television. Something particularly inane and gruesome they will no doubt want to ask you questions about later."

Janice rearranged the cushion behind Walton's head. "Don't worry darling. They'll keep quiet if they know you've got a headache."

"You kidding?" muttered Ethel then went into the kitchen to shovel debris away.

"What did happen Walton?"

Walton looked at Poppy and Bryony for the answer but their expressions implied they were no wiser than he was.

"Odd things keep coming back. I can't make sense of them, though."

But when Walton did start to reconstruct the jigsaw, discretion advised him to keep his mouth shut.

Four wives, the screaming brood he had sired, and two demented poodles ensured that the astronomer's head swam so sickeningly by the time he went to bed that even the tiniest thought was painful.

The next morning it was hours before some semblance of order entered his brain. By now, Walton started to wish he had remained comatose. He wanted to put his recollections down to hallucinations or the hormones that were juggling him through middle age, but a purple-eyed demon kept peering into his mind. He could even have erased the outrageous image of the mother-of-pearl alien given time, but that silver-haired devil had stamped itself on his memory forever. That was the component that convinced him the nightmare had been true. Not even his subconscious could have produced a creature so purringly, implacably malevolent. Perhaps it believed it had burnt his memory out as it had promised. It didn't seem the sort of creature to joke about such a thing.

Janice may have thought her husband had been catapulted into the male menopause by a surfeit of Uncle Arthur's whisky and coffee, but Walton realised how fortunate he was to still find himself sane. Above all, he was sane enough to know better than to tell the story to any self-satisfied scientists like himself. Chunks of it were still missing, but bells rang when he thought of the human race being manipulated by an alien intelligence.

Only hesitating to leave a message for Janice to say he would be home late, Walton called into his laboratory at the college. Then he granted himself a couple of days leave, put through an order for a batch of white mice to be used in gravity and atmospheric experiments. He indented for lead boots and a respirator for the students and then left.

11

Having made some compromise with its irrational existence, the Drune wearily programmed the capsule to take it back up to its demanding mistress. There were a million more entertaining things to do, but Pyg knew a dangerous secret.

Ealinans normally did not use machines to do things they could manage themselves. Why use machines to control experiments on different species when your main joy of life was to wield the cattle prod? The novelty of acquiring an alien android that could do all that and more was too tempting though, even for Pyg. Had the Drune been functioning at its customary efficiency when her crew released it from suspension, it would have known better than to yelp with pain when one of their torches had seared its arm. Without them knowing how it functioned, the Drune would have been in a better position to negotiate terms for its contract of employment, but the knowledge that the android could feel pain had annulled that prospect. So it was compelled to go through these absurd rituals beloved of tyrants, and hope its cinereous skin would come out of it relatively unscorched.

It was sure Pyg sensed how much it hated her. Though not the sort of tyrant who felt insecure enough to demand unswerving devotion, she relished the novelty of a machine with circuits able to feel pain.

"Have you completed your task?" whirred Pyg, as the Drune entered her chamber.

"Yes," it purred in cautious mimicry. "He now has the intellect of a boiled cabbage."

"Clever Drune. You're more efficient than any Ealinan assassin."

"I would have thought your species too businesslike to waste time in genetic diversification."

Pyg suspected the android was inferring that all her race were natural killers and was pretty sure it was not intended as a compliment. "Come here."

The Drune was equally sure about her reaction and hesitated.

"I merely want to see whether you draw your claws when you speak to me."

"If I had any they would ruin my gloves."

"I've never yet met an android who had an expression married to its thoughts. Come here."

The Drune reluctantly approached the dais.

Pyg reached out a spidery arm to touch the Drune, but it backed away. "You know what I'm thinking?"

"You're thinking you would like to dismantle me to see how I work."

"A telepathic Drune."

"But if you did I can promise you I would never work again. Isn't it enough that you can control me?"

"I'm curious to know why I can control you? I want to know why you were only activated when we came back to this planet and broke through to the city above? I'm also curious to know why your creators didn't take you when they deserted it?"

"I frightened them." It gave a malicious snigger. "I might have been constructed as a reservoir for all the unspeakable thoughts their collective subconscious could not cope with."

Pyg was dubious. "The repository of the evil of an entire benign people?"

"Passivity does not construct complexes powerful enough to control an empire. No more does it manipulate molecules to hold apart caverns that have housed generations of Ossianes for millennia, or make robots for its factories and mines. Why do you think you were able to invade so easily? They were without their Drune for so long they lost their defences."

"You did all that?" mocked Pyg.

"That's what they made me for," it lied.

"As well as the vessel for their entire hate?"

"Some mortal minds believe that achievement is degrading to the intellect, yet subconsciously they want that more than anything. In me they had the means of acquiring it and the focus of blame when it was achieved. You can see why they suspended me."

"So what do you want? Sympathy?"

The Drune gave a hollow laugh.

"What then? Revenge?"

The Drune touched its forehead. "Something to make my existence tangible."

"You mean mortality."

"Isn't that the aspiration of all robots?"

"I've met some who knew when they were well off."

"The Ealinan charisma could dampen that sentiment in educated clockwork."

"As passivity does not equate with achievement, practicality encourages survival."

"Practicality can encompass all ability, from operating screwdrivers to annexing planets."

"You already appear to be on the bottom rung of mortality."

"Why?"

"Hypocrisy is usually the first step, Drune. Do you expect me to believe there was never any blood on your hands before we disinterred you? Why else would there have been a plaque on your crystal prison, warning against your release? You would never have been able to carry out my instructions without some previous programming."

The Drune backed away as though the shears were about to descend on its silver mane.

"And why do you need to wear a tunic which baffles any probe we point in your direction?"

"I don't carry my memory with me so your little amphibian was wasting his time."

"Where do you keep it then?"

"Close enough for me to call on, but too deep for you to trace."

"I would like to study your memory, Drune. I suspect you were immobilized for something you deserved to take the blame for."

The Drune gave a resigned sigh. "So I knifed someone. A mere sneeze against the Galactic laws you must have trampled on. Stabbing some stupid creature can hardly be equated with allowing a planet to be pulverized by a comet?"

"But you wanted to be on the edge of the solar system when this planet explodes." The Drune smiled icily. "We won't be sorry either. This world has served its term. If nature has decreed it should disappear, why should we divert the comet?"

"Humans have the technology to stop it, or does evolution demand the decimation of those who can't see through the pollution of their own radio transmissions? Or are you jealous because they are prospering on a planet which decided it had had enough of Ealinans?"

A dangerous expression crept into Pyg's oblong eyes. A germ of malice was glittering too near their diamond-faceted pupils for the Drune's comfort. "You have an aptitude for mortal spite peculiar for a machine."

The Drune said nothing. The ominous whir had returned to Pyg's voice. "You are also inclined to make the mortal mistake of believing most creatures are related in motive, if not physical resemblance."

"Oh, I believe you're an alien. Nothing in that memory your minions have been trying so desperately to discover would dig up a creature more unlikely than you."

"My minions?" whirred Pyg. "They're merely things of amusement to you aren't they."

"Ealinan evolution couldn't have been that practical when it coughed them up."

"Why do you mock my Captain and his crew?"

"Me? Mock your frogs?"

The germ of malice in Pyg's eyes bloomed into a dangerous sparkle. The Drune probably knew the danger in sneering, but did so all the same.

"They're idiots. I can't help it if they're scared to death of the sight of me."

"You regularly feed the scout craft false data and jam the bay door. You know they hate swimming from the escape hatch."

"It doesn't harm them."

"You don't know what the word harm means."

"And you're going to educate me?"

"Ealinans have this morbid tendency called self esteem. My crew may be the dregs of some evolutionary pond to you, but you will not treat any of our species with contempt."

"Most 'advanced' species must have the same problem."

"What a pity for you that the next rung to mortality

you've managed to climb is pain." Pyg raised the palm of her hand. Strapped to it was a flashing button.

The Drune now realised it had not been summoned for mere conversation. "No." It backed away carefully. "I'll leave your pet frogs alone if that's what you want. You'll damage me if you keep doing that."

To make sure it couldn't run off Pyg pressed the control, which slammed the chamber shutter.

"I'll programme a charm school's curriculum into my circuits. Stun me and it'll be another drain on your energy and spoil your looks."

"So you think I'm beautiful, do you?"

"I'll programme in the right reply to that as well."

"You're not going to have the chance to reach your memory."

"So what should an artificial neuter designed by a different species say?"

"Sorry Drune. Very, very sorry."

"But I am."

"No, you silver snake. I meant I'm sorry."

"No creature with its mouth under its chin can apologize convincingly."

"Then what should I say, Drune? 'Tormenting you gives me as much pleasure as you get from tormenting others'? Look upon this reprimand as being good for the soul your evil existence will never acquire."

"But I don't know why I'm wicked. Why should it have to be my fault?"

"I never said it was. I am saying that, whatever you do to the hominids, you will treat us with respect."

"But I'm never rude to any of you."

"Don't take me for a fool, Drune."

The Drune did not. Like a black dart it sprang across the chamber to keep out of the button's range. Pyg wasn't bothered; the extra target practice kept her reflexes in trim.

She depended on the creature for too many things so she turned down the weapon's power. She couldn't afford to permanently damage it.

The Drune would have taken refuge in the cryogenic chamber but Pyg had sealed the door to that as well. It tried to dash up the steps to the gallery. Before it was half way there Pyg had it in her sights. A bright burst of energy blew it from its perch. The Drune toppled to the floor where it writhed in agony for a few seconds.

"Well Drune." It eventually showed signs of being able to hear her. "Perhaps you would like to tell me the real reason for your suspension?"

The Drune's eyes flashed an illogical defiance. Whatever it was about to do, Pyg raised the palm of her hand to warn against it.

"I stabbed their Chief Technical Adviser." There was no remorse in its tone. "They thought it was a serious crime, but the creature was a deluded idiot."

Pyg was oddly delighted at the revelation. "So you *are* dangerous. Why did you do it?"

"It was the logical solution for a deluded idiot."

"I suspect you only engage in logic when it best suits you? You're a malicious contrivance aren't you," she laughed. "You've no cause to be so proud."

"I was never programmed to grovel."

"Oh, I'll make you grovel before long. Finding a way to do so will keep me amused."

"Please don't lose any sleep over it on my account. Or do reptiles like you only need a short nap every month at 200 degrees below?"

Pyg instantly stunned the Drune.

"Call me a reptile again and I'll have you pleading to be destroyed."

"Even you couldn't live long enough to work out how to do that," the Drune eventually gasped.

"I shall accept that as a challenge. Now," Pyg relaxed. "I think our little conversation is finished. You may go." The Drune seemed reluctant to rise. "Stop overacting. That was only a low burst."

She opened the chamber shutter. The Drune managed to get up and stagger to it. After watching the android's pained movements, Pyg tapped several keys on her monitor. Since her mouth was hidden under her chin, had the Drune looked back, it would not have noticed her amused expression. Perhaps it was not as clever as it thought after all.

As the pain subsided, the Drune became even more angry. It could hardly go back and punch Pyg on a nose she did not have, so it decided to pay someone else a visit. Someone who never fought back. It entered a lift cage and slumped into a corner to think as it travelled upwards.

As the lift was passing by, several lights in Rosipolees, the city above Pyg's complex, sparkled into life. After a few moments a cleansing unit stopped scrubbing the mould of condensation from an archway and turned to listen to the pumpkin shaped statue perched on the end of a balustrade.

"Been arguing again, I bet."

The mobile cleanser was not programmed to gossip, but was bored. After so many centuries of scraping moulds and mosses from the deserted walkways and malls in Rosipolees, any conversation was a novelty.

"Can't understand it myself," the statue went on in the computer language that was common to both of them. "You'd think they'd get on after all this while."

The cleanser lowered its brush for a moment. "Don't see why the grey creature has anything to do with those aliens. They're not up to any good, you know."

"Well, they leave us alone, I suppose. Between you and me, I don't think they know we're active."

"Why not?"

"Well, if the Drune hasn't told them and we keep our voices down, why should it occur to them."

"See what you mean. Think they'd switch us off if they did find out?"

"They'd have to immobilize the city computer, and without her the shielding would buckle." The statue flushed a malicious pink. "They can't shut off any of the other city computers either."

"No, really?"

"The Drune granted them all control of their own shielding before the aliens knew anything about it. Everything would collapse if they tried to tamper with them."

Both the units started to snigger until something occurred to the cleanser. "That's not funny."

The statue turned an apologetic green. "No, I don't suppose it is. Between you and me, I don't really have that much time for mortals but I can't say I want to see them flattened either."

"I don't even like increases in pressure. They bend the bristles on my brush."

"You should see what they do to the insides of the larger conversation pieces. Spill all over the place they do."

The cleanser rattled in annoyance. "Don't tell me. We're the ones who have to refill them and clear up the mess, and that fluid is corrosive, you know. It may make them turn pretty colours, but once it hits the pavement we have to call out building units to fill in the holes."

"Well, the city computer's trying to realign the shielding. It's apparently something to do with the molecular bonding; some molecules aren't lining up as straight as others."

The cleanser shook the mould from its brush. "Don't try and explain it to me. I only do the sweeping up around here." Its fund of conversation exhausted for another year, the unit gathered up its bucket and trundled off.

The pumpkin-shaped statue turned a dark mauve and went back to sleep.

12

Rabette was bustling about, ordering capsules back to their stations and checking the seals of pressure locks. He was so consumed by his task he did not notice the sinister black-clad figure watching him with calculated interest.

"Why so industrious, little brother?" the Drune purred.

Rabette leapt in alarm. "What do you want?"

"Nothing. It's just a friendly visit."

Rabette managed to kick Akaylia's satchel under a couch without the Drune noticing, and then he desperately tried to think of some ploy to make it leave.

"You haven't come up here just to be sarcastic have you?"

"But of course. Why so reluctant to see your best friend?"

"I hardly have enough other company to be choosy." Rabette realised that Akaylia's shawl was hanging a short distance above their heads, its fringe dancing dangerously in the circulating air from the entrance.

"How drained you look little brother. Did you have a close call in that magma chamber?"

"Very."

"Why didn't you call me? You know I'm less destructible."

"Real people have sentiments called self esteem, though I would hardly expect you to know about real feelings."

The Drune sighed as it sensed the possibility it might have to rerun the previous discussion that had left it doubled up in agony.

"How real do I have to become to satisfy you?"

"You could never be real enough to satisfy me. You're an android and can't be anything else."

"Would you like to know how to switch me off?"

"You'd tell me that?" Rabette scoffed.

"Come to my lab and I might."

"What?" This alarmed Rabette, then he saw the shawl slowly slipping from its pipe.

"I have something to show you."

There was nothing else for it. Rabette gritted his teeth. "All right."

The Drune sensed it should have been more suspicious at the Atlantian's sudden sociability, but was satisfied enough that the invitation had been accepted.

Not looking forward to the journey at all, Rabette switched the control onto automatic monitor and sprinted through the entrance after the Drune just as the fluttering fringe cascaded to the floor. Obstinately insisting on taking his own capsule, he allowed the Drune to programme the route to depths that would intimidate even his subterranean experience. He dare not protest when the android switched off the vehicle's inside lights. As dimly lit tunnels and cavernous chambers rushed past, Rabette watched the Drune's flashing purple eyes in reluctant fascination. He hated himself for being intimidated by the creature. He wished it could have been flesh enough to understand the discomfort it caused him.

"Why can't we have some light?" he eventually managed to pluck up the courage to ask.

"We do not need light for what I have to show you little

brother. There is no reason to be alarmed. There is very little light in the vast emptiness of the Universe. The dark is comforting to creatures like me."

The capsule started to descend with alarming speed.

Rabette realised that they weren't heading for the laboratory he knew. "Where are we going?"

"To my other home. No one else knows anything about it."

Then Rabette lost his nerve. "Take me back."

"Patience, little friend. There is nothing down here to hurt you. All my volcanic dragons are tame."

"I'm not an android. This capsule wasn't designed for these depths."

"The tunnels are safe. I excavated them myself."

"What for? You already have a base."

"Presently you will see."

Rabette was by then quite sure he didn't want to but, as they were propelled under some massive shutters that slammed down behind them, the sentiment was redundant.

They disembarked into a world of eerie half-light. Some passages were so dim Rabette was tempted to cling to the Drune's arm but he knew what its reaction would be to that.

"Why isn't there more light?"

"I don't want to be seen," was the enigmatic reply. "I like the half light."

"I can't see where I'm going."

The Drune opened a shutter, which revealed a wonderland of flickering, spinning, dancing lights. Pinpricks of different colours were the complex's only illumination, but at least Rabette was able to avoid walking into an array of equipment. Even his subterranean world had nothing like this. Funnels, spiralling tubes, fans of crystal filled with condensing fluids, transparent boxes with counters ticking away processions of binary numbers and jars full of gurgling gases filled corners and littered benches. Pressure gauges, alien gravimeters and rotating gyroscopes surrounded a large three-dimensional plan of their solar system. The blazing sun, although small, was frighteningly real, like a living hologram.

To keep Rabette's fascination from rising to alarm, the Drune handed him a small panel of polished opal. When he turned it, the light caught in its many facets shone back an intricate pattern. The material may have been natural but the way it had been worked certainly was not.

"Where did you get this?"

"My home."

"Your home?" Rabette was puzzled. "You make it sound as though you come from a different planet?"

"Would you like to see Avacynth?"

"Is that why you brought me down here?"

"I would like you to see Avacynth."

"All right," Rabette agreed cautiously, knowing he was not in a position to refuse. "But don't take too long. I don't like leaving things on automatic."

The Drune beckoned its trembling guest to a large sphere covered by a shroud as black as its tunic. Carefully it lifted the cover away. Rabette was dazzled by the sudden radiance pulsating from the globe. It swam with a milky fluorescence in which brilliant bubbles expanded and shrank as though waiting for instructions to take shape. The light dappled the Drune's satanic presence as it lifted its hands. The globe slowly cleared. Images started to form.

The impossible dimensions displayed in its depths entranced Rabette. The beauty of this otherworld was stupefying, its clarity and alien appearance was somehow familiar. There was nothing frightening about the vision, apart from the people – only they weren't people. This island was inhabited by androids like the Drune. There seemed to be thousands of the creatures; all elegant, all different. Had Rabette not known the population of Avacynth were androids he would have been overcome by admiration instead of trepidation.

On this pristine pinnacle punctuating a satin blue sea, ancient artefacts melded pleasingly with the more functional buildings. Avacynth appeared to not only have a history, but a future as well.

The image in the screen led them into the colonnaded cloister of a vibrant hall. Coruscating curtains of mobile sculptures created the shimmering movements that filled its interior. There were rippling fans made from fronds of gleaming metal, sheets of gold and silver studded with pearls and ruby, and tiger's eye blossomed into flowers nature would have been proud to design. Streamers of diamonds fluttered in rotation like eternal snowflakes, never quite settling, but making speckled flashes in the forest of mineral vegetation. Rabette was so consumed with the images it did not cross his mind to wonder what the hall might be, let alone why androids would have needed such an elaborate celebration of peculiarly mortal skills.

Out of the hall the Drune led his dazed vision, through a complex of avenues, bowers and squares covered by stained glass glinting in a bright sun. Who could have built Avacynth? Perhaps the creators of the androids? Perhaps the androids were as much part of the decoration as the statuary, fountains of wrought iron and exotic fruiting trees? But this paradise was only the fantasy from the machine's mind.

Rabette suddenly felt himself snatched up and carried out over the vast sea. He could sense the satanic sorcerer by his elbow as they rapidly rotated with thunder clouds, were dazzled by forks of lightning and hurled back down with the storm's torrent. For an Atlantian, this above world experience was terrifying. It may have been the Drune's idea of a joke, but Rabette did not need to turn to know it still wore that frozen mask of amiable deceit.

When they reached a continent's rim, their landing was cushioned by billows of burgeoning branches. The inhabitants of the trees paid no attention to their clumsy arrival and carried on preening, chattering and nesting. Without so much as rippling the leaves, the Drune carried the startled Rabette through the foliage and over meadows cladding hillsides, and dells of woodland. Gossamer gliders slid silently between huge balloons that faintly thrummed below them. Whether over land or water, everything floated, making noiseless dents in nature's design.

They passed a hillside so pitted with caves it looked like a mound of pink Emmenthal. Faces peered from entrances as though anticipating some life-threatening menace. They were human, but too primitive to be designers of the wheel let alone androids, and looking so alien in their strange wilderness that Rabette involuntarily shuddered, glad to pass them by. Once again, Rabette was swept upwards. He fancied his fingers grasped the Drune's ruff of hair in terror, half-afraid it would let him fall, half-afraid it was still there. This time they were heading into the future, even the planets. Without time to put his fear in a spacesuit, Rabette was able to look back at the oxygen blue of a world his ancestors would have industriously burrowed into. Its silver crescent moon hung like a spangle as it descended in its orbit and a distant comet had just started to have its plume breathed into life by the solar wind.

"What's that?" asked Rabette.

"A large comet travelling this way," said the Drune. But Rabette was descended from excavators not astronomers. The thought passed when something horrific plunged from the star-seeded blackness. As they hung suspended against the backdrop of space a gleaming monster was silently pushing its malevolent way towards them. Rabette could hear voices. He covered his ears, only to find that the sound was in his head. His mind tried to escape back to the safety of the chamber but he was compelled to watch a gargantuan body fill his field of view. It eventually blocked out the asteroids, the planets and the sun, until there was nothing but the implications it had melded into his mind. Those layers of fantasy his brain had been able to accept were obliterated. It was now filled with terrifying truths he could not name.

Feeling his sanity about to be crowded out, Rabette did the only thing open to him under the circumstances. He panicked. He panicked so frenziedly he managed to break free and flee from the Drune's chamber.

Wrenched from the illusion too rapidly, the Drune was disorientated and toppled over. It sprang up in alarm to pursue Rabette but a warning light flashed. Rabette would have to wait. It dare not ignore the summons from Commander Pyg's ship. Her pet frogs, the Ealinans that crewed it, knew the android was still smarting from the reprimand for tormenting them.

13

Rabette left the Drune's laboratory in such a fearful panic it was some while before he stopped to wonder where he was going. Knowing he must have been at the bottom of the planet's crust and only surviving through the benevolence of the plastic moho, he trod the buttressed chambers gingerly. Though he was an inquisitive mortal, a situation like this could have dampened a cat's curiosity. He wanted to find his way up and out – and fast, but there was no obvious route to pursue. In this maze the passages could have led anywhere.

After the fright the Drune had given him, Rabette was too scared to go back to its laboratory, but then to his relief the light ahead increased. From a wide well a spotlight was stabbing through the gloom. As Rabette looked up he found himself gazing into a wide black chasm ascending into heights he could only guess at.

What would the Drune want a hole like that for? It must have reached the planet's surface. As he peered into the illuminated pit below, the terrible truth became apparent. Rabette did not want to admit it to himself. He had often assumed the Drune to be constructed from several layers of playful malevolence but at the core having some spark of mortality, however small. The horror below him belied that hope.

Planted securely on its launch pad was a rocket. Not just a straightforward warhead, but a sufficient amalgamation of missiles to lay waste the planet's surface. They were carefully welded to a booster capable of reaching the other side of the solar system.

Rabette suspected the Drune had never really liked humans, but this was taking dislike too far. He descended into the silo, hoping to discover some unguarded connection he might sabotage. Perhaps a gyroscope could be tampered with to make the monster collide with the walls of the tunnel? Even the resulting earthquake would be less devastating than the world-wide fallout. But, as the Drune had often assured him, its thinking was infallible. Most of the circuitry was welded in, and he couldn't make sense of any connections that weren't.

He now began to curse himself for accepting the wretched creature's invitation. It would have been preferable if the Drune had discovered Akaylia's shawl. If it had come to verbal or physical combat, she could have outweighed the android on both counts. As there was no way to foil the Drune's infernal design, it might have been better if Armageddon came as a surprise; but his race had invested too much energy engineering the planet's crust away from its most destructive inclinations.

Although Rabette hardly knew them, the impulse to preserve all the species above was too great. There was no point in practicing to be a human being if the Drune obliterated them. Safe as the last Atlantians may have been in their sanitized depths, it had to be stopped.

Rabette hastily clambered out of the silo and doubled back along the route he had taken. He was relieved the Drune had not chased after him but, aware of its reasoning, knew it could have been waiting, spider-like, to pounce from any dark crevice or cranny. Cold urgency dampened Rabette's instinct to panic. Somehow he managed to find the courage to open the shutters of the Drune's laboratory.

The air was cloaked in eerie silence, but he had to go in. There was nowhere else he could find the controls for that massive shutter which shielded the complex from the prying Universe. Rabette's sight was now accustomed to the dimness and his technician's eye started to make sense of the indicator lights. A battery of panels against a slanting wall appeared to be the terminal for intercepting signals from another location. They resembled the equipment in the Drune's other laboratory. A message had been relayed to the unit and attended to so rapidly it had not been erased.

Rabette sighed with relief. That meant the Drune had left the complex. He replayed the communication. It was verbal, though in a language incomprehensible to him. As the clicking of a thin tongue spelt out some demand Rabette felt the roots of his hair crackle in terror. It was not a human voice. The Drune must have been in league with aliens. Aliens about to destroy the Earth?

Though the Drune had never presented itself as a trustworthy friend, Rabette felt betrayed and angry. If it had to be evil why couldn't it have been more recognizably diabolical about it. Then another possibility dawned. Perhaps it had been planted here by the aliens in the first place? Their appearance would have probably alarmed the Atlantians so they might have depended on this reasoning machine to do their engineering for them. There was no other Drune and it was remarkably adept at tunnelling.

Rabette swiftly toured the chamber looking for the main shutter control but came to the large globe first. Burning with anxiety to leave, something rooted him to the spot. What about Avacynth? How could a machine have the imagination to picture an island inhabited by its own kind? Why should it need to be reassured by the sight of such a never-never land?

Not knowing he had the courage, Rabette gingerly picked up a corner of the black cover. He tugged the material gently, and it slipped from the large sphere. A sudden light throbbed into the chamber. He tried to recall how the Drune had raised the images. It had concentrated. There was probably a signal it used to switch on the pictures.

Rabette lifted his hands and concentrated not expecting, nor hoping for, any result. He was apparently more adept than he guessed. The bubbles of brightness lost their comforting roundness to take on sinister amoebic shapes. From them peered a pair of oblong eyes. Rabette knew that this should have warned him off, but as the apparition formed, terror nailed him to the spot. He found himself looking at an alien.

It was not simian. Evolution had been working on this design for far longer than Atlantians or humans. Everything about it was a celebration of bland economy. No hair, no scales, no nails, no decorative relief of any kind. Was that thing living in the back of his mind? The thought made him snatch up the cover and throw it over the creature. Then he remembered he had once dreamt about such a spectre. Could his bubbling senses be deceiving him? Perhaps there was no rocket or alien message. Perhaps the Drune had been playfully driving him mad; he now believed it was malevolent enough. He didn't know what to think. He wasn't used to such intellectual pondering. The illusion might pass when he was safely in his own quarters.

Rabette's reeling senses did not prevent him from finding the main shutter control. With confused agility he darted out of the complex and tumbled thankfully into his capsule. The Drune had left his return route in the automatic pilot. Without wondering why, Rabette activated it and lay back in exhausted relief as it carried him home.

14

After pacing so many miles of featureless tunnel, Akaylia started to feel more like a mole than a geologist. Air conditioning or not, the temperature was still oppressive enough to daunt her reams of ample flesh. She could feel it vaporizing ounce by ounce as her deodorant was washed away in rivulets of perspiration, the sticky glow saturating every fold and crevice making her very aware of the laws of gravity and her confident stride turning into a laboured amble. That increase in pressure may have been due to another volcano squatting in burbling anticipation on top of the complex but, having come so far, nothing short of its eruption would have made her turn back.

In the distance was a light that had a different hue to the more subtle illumination of the Atlantian world. Its harshness gleamed through an archway. Suddenly it flashed off, then on again. In the brief darkness Akaylia could see rows of spangled lights.

The Drune rechecked the launch sequence for Pyg's ship. Its Captain was more jumpy than usual after Walton's visit and another flux in transmission strength. The android would have preferred to work in the gloom but Pyg's mortal eyes were not able to keep watch on her domain in the dark and Ealinans found other wavelengths tedious to use; a penalty for too much evolution.

Having finished dealing with Pyg's crew, the Drune went to the monitor for the main storage memory and briefly watched a new flow of information. One civil war, thousands starve in arid wasteland that had once been fertile paddy fields, another treaty proposed on ballistic missiles – neither side being totally sure the other wasn't stealing theirs – a football crowd that had become hysterical, with fifteen trampled to death and 182 injured and so on, all collated and translated into figures for transmission home. What fun the Ealinans were having with their white mice.

The arch sensors suddenly bleated. The Drune snapped off the monitor, then spun round to discover the perspiring, panting Akaylia beaming in delight. Had it been possible to give the android a nasty fright, Akaylia's sudden appearance would have fused a few of its circuits. For several moments its reflexes were immobilized. It even lost the presence of mind to reach out and switch off Pyg's monitor.

Eventually it found the wit to look fierce. "Who are you?"

But Akaylia was not easily intimidated. She ambled leisurely into its chamber with a cool premeditation that denied her sweltering condition.

"A robot," she chortled.

"I possess reason," it cautioned her.

"A reasoning robot."

"Do not come any closer." It was intended as a threat but sounded more like panic.

"Oh hourglass of silken silver gossamer, what majestic hand fanned out that moonburst of shimmering sensuous strands. What metaphysical mentor could have chiselled that satanic silhouette, that cleverly cross profile, that wickedly willing glance?"

The Drune looked amazed but Akaylia went on regardless.

"Why have you been planted in these craterous depths? To grow from the murmuring moho and burst through the planet's crust in an eruption of icy slivers?"

Watching on her monitor, Pyg was also baffled by the eccentric's arrival and was inclined to assume that, though clearly mad, the woman seemed reasonably harmless. She found the android's reaction more interesting. For the first time since she had encountered it, the machine was at a loss for words – but Akaylia's had far from run out.

"What an amazing skin your maker chose you to live in! Tell me your name, scintillating, synthetic simian."

"I am a Drune," it declared frostily.

"If I knew what sex you were meant to be I could fancy you, though given the way I look I don't suppose I should be fussy."

The Drune continued to view the plump arrival with suspicion. "Who are you?"

"Akaylia Jackson, failed potholer, oh casket of tantalizing titillation."

"How did you get down here?"

"I chased a white rabbit down a hole."

"I will show you the way back up."

"But I've no appointments for which I'm going to be late. Let me stay down here, while I'm losing weight."

"And it is a gruesome sight."

"Oh wonder of wonders; an adroit android, a riposting robot, a witty . . ."

"Drune."

"Drune," she mused. "A dainty Drune, a discoursing Drune . . . a distinctly unsociable Drune." She reached out to touch its mane but it leapt back. "Why, what wonders would be revealed by one hair from that magnificent mop? Secret knowledge of the Ancients perhaps? What manner of forbidden fruit is yet untasted by a middle-aged misfit like myself? What wonders must remain interred with this mysterious machine under so many tons of brutal basalt, black and burning in bottomless foreboding?"

"Most of them are now flat and you'd never be able to crawl into the cracks with your figure."

"Doesn't the pressure sit heavily on your circuits, Drune?"

"No, but magnetism can play havoc with my sense of balance. It can also make me violent and sporadically burst into flame. I can feel an attack coming on now."

"I don't mind you smoking if you want to."

"Are you really sure you wouldn't like to go away? How many layers of fat can you afford to lose in this heat?"

"Such command in those creamy contralto tones. Insinuating, yet invidious; mellifluous, yet menacing."

"I would much prefer not to fascinate you. Perhaps I could find your white rabbit? I assume he was the one to bring you this deep?"

"I never got here through a pothole, passion pacifier."

"I will speak to him about this."

"That tone bodes bother for the milky moppet?"

"Humans fascinate him. He hardly has the chance to meet any. He sometimes thinks he is one even though his race decided to tunnel away from the species millennia ago."

"Why did you decide to live in a burrow then? What imperious paw programmed you to dwell beneath the magma chambers and mighty machinery moulding magnificent mountains?"

"I like the view."

"If I owned you I would have you suspended in crystal, packed in clear plastic, even delineated in diamond, not chancing a squashed Drune down here."

With startling swiftness Akaylia pressed her palm onto

the Drune's chest. Having been backed against a wall it was unable to leap aside this time. The fabric of its dense black tunic creaked uneasily and the Drune's eyes opened wide in alarm.

"Wouldn't you like to be *my* Drune?" Akaylia increased the pressure. "A dutiful Drune. A doting delicious delight to this disproportionately designed damsel? Or perhaps your owner would be jealous, mega muppet?"

The Drune could virtually feel Pyg's eyes taking in every detail of the encounter. "Very."

"Perhaps she would clip your mane and tie a knot in your tail?"

"Probably."

"Spoil your looks, demonic delicacy?"

"Undoubtedly."

"Shame. I need an android to do the housework."

"Please go . . ."

"Being watched are we?"

"Please go."

"Just to indulge you, pretty parcel. Don't know where I could find some sodium chloride, do you?"

"What for?"

"I like salt on rabbit."

"No. But if you promise to go, I will tell Rabette to meet you."

"Promise?"

"He will. He's afraid of me."

Before the Drune could avoid it, Akaylia pulled out several strands of its hair and waved them like a trophy as she sauntered from sight.

Pyg carefully observed the disorientating effect of the encounter on her lackey and opened transmission as soon as she was out of earshot. "Why didn't you stop the human and erase her memory?"

"I don't think she would have liked the idea."

"Fool!"

"All right, I'll send her down for you to sort out."

"Don't you dare. Time's getting short. We can't waste it playing games with the wildlife."

The Drune gave a sharp laugh. "Anyway, she's the sort of person other humans wouldn't take seriously even if she did manage to escape before you go."

"All right. Get your pet Rabette to take her out of here. I don't want that human wandering near the matrix. You will have to reprimand him for bringing her down."

"It might make him more suspicious."

"That creature doesn't have the nerve to be suspicious. It's already frightened of you. Just make it fear you a little more."

The Drune did as it was ordered. It gave Rabette's control the co-ordinates of the happily ambling anomaly meandering through tunnels a Drune's whisker away from crushing incineration.

Instead of fetching Akaylia, Rabette sent her a capsule programmed to take her to any part of the underground complex she desired to visit, plus enough food and drink to keep her appetite satisfied for several days. He knew she would soon find her way back when the food and curiosity ran out. Then he got on with his task of contacting the other Atlantians.

15

Walton Clarke parked his car in a concealing nook at the bottom of the range of hills. Careful to avoid coming into view of Uncle Arthur's bungalow, he climbed the steep slope.

As before, the place was deserted. Poppy's grumpy Uncle was probably the best protection the aliens had from UFO spotters. Given the clumsy way his rheumatic fingers handled a double-barrelled shotgun, even the neighbouring farm's cows knew better than to graze their way onto his land.

After many stumbles on the rocky descent, Walton reached the shore of the lake. The trigger that activated the entrance to the hill had been moved. He eventually found a likely looking mound of pebbles set close to the rock-face. Nearby was a prominence he could hide behind when the inquisitive scout ship came up to see who had rung the bell.

Taking no chances, Walton selected a large boulder and hurled it onto the pebbles. A second later he was well hidden. He heard the grinding of shutters inside, then they abruptly stopped. Not seeing any movement from the lake he stepped out from his hiding place. The entrance had been opened just wide enough to let him squeeze through. Now

Walton was able to see what had caused the light he had glimpsed the last time.

He was standing on a narrow walkway just below the domed ceiling of a vast chamber. Arched buttresses hundreds of feet high were supporting the hill above. Like segments of an inverted orange, they enclosed the most peculiar fruit imaginable. It must have been a mile in circumference and lights buzzed busily on and off all over its gleaming metallic skin. Small UFOs Walton could now easily cope with, but the sight of this monster made him quake.

The activity below suggested that the star cruiser was going through some sort of countdown sequence. Walton could see why no scout ship had come out to investigate the intruder. They were being stowed in the great craft's underbelly. But how had this cosmic intrusion into the countryside gone unnoticed? Just as the thought crossed his mind the entrance behind him closed. Now he had to find a way down. The place was so vast even he was just a speck on the ceiling, but he was more afraid of becoming a smudge on the floor.

Slowly Walton eased himself along the narrow ledge in the hope of finding a better route. He was on the verge of turning back to try his luck in the other direction when the wall he was pressed against suddenly vanished. With several curses of terror he tumbled down an uneven slope. He managed to look up in time to see the wall seal itself just as rapidly.

Not immediately wanting to know who or what had made the invitation, Walton pulled himself up and limped a short way down a dimly lit passage. This excavation was much more ancient than the spaceship's dock. It didn't seem to be the accurate handiwork of the Drune so perhaps he had accidentally triggered a rusting latch. Either way, it was preferable to waiting to be found on the other side.

Walton spiralled his way down through the ancient tunnels for some distance. He was puzzled because the air seemed cleaner down there than above. It must have been wafted up by giant bellows. Although the ceilings were uncomfortably low for his height the walls were widely spaced as though the inhabitants had either been very short and fat or they usually traversed them in some sort of vehicle.

Somewhere in the distance the astronomer heard voices. They seemed human but were talking in a foreign tongue. He waited cautiously in the hope of seeing their owners before they saw him, but unfortunately his size was not on his side. Before Walton could retreat, two extremely white faces suddenly confronted him, gazing up at him in amazement. It was difficult to tell who had startled whom the most.

"Hallo," he eventually said, to try to distract the two small women's embarrassing observation of him.

"Hallo," one of them replied.

"You speak my language?"

"Some speak. Anniya speak better." The female indicated her companion who was still gawping at the intruder. "We listen. You speak?"

"I'm lost." It was obvious they had already deduced that, so he went on. "You've not come across a creature called a 'Drune' have you?"

That did have a galvanizing effect.

"Drune no Atlantian."

"You mean – you're actually . . . ?"

Walton was quite sure he had just picked up another one way ticket to a rest home.

"Anniya explain. Come."

Walton followed the rapid pace of the two women. Anniya was eventually able to communicate, answering his first question.

"The Drune is dangerous. We have lived peacefully down here with it for a long while and, although it is mischievous, it has never harmed any of us. But we have just learnt something terrible about it."

"Well?" Walton prompted.

"It has excavated a complex deep in the crust. After stealing several missiles and a rocket from above, it has constructed a massive multiple warhead."

"Oh my God!"

"You believe us?"

"I've met the creature. I believe you."

"Is it possible it could have built such a missile then?"

"With the right warheads, very possible."

"This is what Rabette insists. He claims it is fully fuelled and ready for launch."

"We've got to stop it."

"We wish we knew how."

"What did this friend of yours tell you?"

"Only that he has an idea. When we reach a capsule bay we will be able to go to him."

"Well let's get a move on then."

The capsule they first encountered had not been designed for bodies of Walton's proportions. By the time they reached their destination he felt like a cod packed into a sardine tin.

They eventually docked in a landing bay already filled with similar vehicles. Some were customized to cater for individual tastes, from the psychedelic to virtually invisible. The astronomer was suddenly apprehensive about the fact he hadn't seen any traffic lights. He assumed by their cavalier attitude to safety that was the reason they were a dying race.

Being the last to arrive, Walton's entry was something of a surprise. A row of pale faces gawped up at his towering presence as though he were an acrobat leaping out of a sack.

Eventually the novelty wore off and they parted to let him through to a small, animated man wearing a tartan suit and hairstyle like the uncontrolled explosion of a pillow.

"Are you the brother of Akaylia?" he asked.

Walton cracked his head on the lintel as he entered the room. "Who?"

"If you are looking for her, she departed in a capsule ages ago."

"I haven't got a sister."

"Oh." Rabette realised it was a silly question. Akaylia was black, where Walton was white. And then again she would have probably pushed any other siblings from the nest like a rapacious cuckoo chick.

Anniya rapidly explained Walton's quest to the others. Heads nodded in approval.

"You could help us capture the Drune?" Rabette asked. "You know it is an android?"

"Yes, but I reckon I know how to disorientate it. It could be very risky of course. The only thing is, I wouldn't know what to do with it when we have it."

"Rabette has an idea," Anniya told Walton. "This is the laboratory our ancestors used to service robots and androids. We seldom use it now. Our cities are uninhabited and only need essential maintenance."

Walton tried to guess the function of the ancient equipment, but would have had better luck in the den of a Chinese alchemist. For all he knew, Drunes were grown from magic crystals snatched from the moho; it was difficult to imagine one containing circuit boards or chips. He was beginning to have the feeling that sorcery was involved, a sure sign he was getting out of his depth. It was the same sensation those bloody art students gave him.

Anniya led Walton into another room. He hit his head again.

Then she pointed to an adjoining chamber. "Through

there is a medical centre. That is always kept stocked. Down here accidents are frequent. This room is where we keep the benches used for dismantling android units."

Walton shuddered at the idea for some reason. "What's that yellow and black fur in this indentation?"

"Probably a post wasp. They always put up a fight."

The astronomer was even less inclined to know any more about it, but that wasn't businesslike. "How does it work?"

"The unit was placed on the bench and held in position over the grid," Rabette explained. "From beneath a jolt of power was sent through its body to detect and disrupt any faulty circuits. This way, all defective parts were burnt out and those still usable easily removed and recycled. The unit had to be very defective of course."

"The Drune wouldn't be too happy about us calling it that. Does the equipment still work?"

"I have been adapting it. Like everything down here it's ancient but will operate effectively enough to dismember the Drune. Our main problem will be capturing it."

"I don't know which I will enjoy more."

Rabette didn't seem so enthusiastic about the exercise so Walton told him, "You will have to take me to it."

"I suppose I must."

"And I'll need everyone here to help me sit on it."

"How dangerous do you think it is?"

"Very, but if I'm right, we can confuse its co-ordination."

"What happens if we can't overpower it?"

"You'd better hold your noses. I've strange feeling there could be an overpowering smell of burning flesh."

16

Down and down, round and round, Akaylia gleefully darted her capsule through the honeycomb maze. Every now and then she took a detour to meander about some bizarre half-lit city. None of chambers held the complex she was looking for. The one she wanted seemed to have fallen off the edge of Rabette's map, as though relegated to the realms of fantasy and a badly printed fiche.

Soon losing interest in the supplies he had sent, Akaylia started to crave more exotic food, perhaps a few truffles and fresh subterranean mango. Some corn on the cob would have gone down well but the only specimens she had encountered so far in the occasional farm were chequered red and white, something, in its raw state, even her appetite would have had difficulty coping with. But the hunger pangs grew, possibly because of the same rogue hormone that occasionally made her crave black olives and kumquat sandwiches. At the next farm she discovered a better colour co-ordinated version of the maize in orange and cream. Snatching several heads of corn through the capsule window she took them to the adjoining city where a civic hot spring bubbled erratically before a rambling building on the verge of decay. All the springs down there were warm, but this one gave off enough steam to broil an ox. Akaylia found a reel of safety line in the back of Rabette's capsule and used it to lower the cobs into the water as she floated several feet above it. The sauna and shards of colour glinting in the half-light should have been relaxing, but her stomach juices were not the only things rumbling warnings. Her eardrums started to throb. A woman her age should have been used to palpitations, but it soon became apparent that the source was external.

Carefully securing the thread holding the corn, Akaylia looked through the rear window and saw a massive wasp. She turned back to check the food in the hope the apparition would be gone by the time she restored her attention, but it hadn't. It hung there, glowering and throbbing with anger as though it had forgotten how to buzz. Akaylia used the console to call up the general translation programme Rabette had supplied. There was nothing on wasps, though there were several paragraphs on bees. Then she noticed it was wearing a hat. Something was written on it in bold letters but she didn't recognize any of them. She called up the dictionary. Apparently the wasp was a post insect, which explained the small satchel hanging from its pollen-coated midriff. As its wings whirred she realised that the halo which surrounded it was the dust of centuries and not some ghostly emanation.

"Good grief," Akaylia muttered to herself. "It can't have a message for me – can it?"

Cautiously she leaned out of the window and beckoned it round. It zigzagged to her side in a blur. With a few brief clicks and whirrs the wasp reached into its satchel and pulled out a solitary letter. Akaylia thanked the machine and gingerly took it from its mandible. In the next instant it had gone.

She turned the envelope over several times, not really wanting to know what was inside it. Even if the wasp had looked more friendly and buzzed like an amiable bumble-bee, insect deliveries seemed an inappropriate way to convey good news. But there was her name scrawled in an elegant, hasty hand.

She opened it and read,

Akaylia Jackson,

I hope you are as mad as you appear. Things down here are getting out of hand and you might be crazy enough to come to grips with them.

A computer with an illogic circuit, which I have no doubt you could plug into, runs the lowest level city. After all this time without conversation she'll probably talk to anyone.

Enclosure: One map to Rosipolees, in detail.

PS. If you are unable to oblige, world will end in approximately five and a half months. See you then.

"Only approximately?" thought Akaylia. It wasn't like the sender to be so unspecific. She sighed. It looked as though her corn on the cob would have to wait. She pulled up the half-done vegetables and took a token nibble. It tasted very good. So she finished them up before propping the map up on the console. Akaylia dare not risk trying to programme the route so she gingerly took the controls and headed downwards once more.

17

The Drune glanced up at the reflection of an annoyed face in its control panel and switched off Pyg's monitor.

"Dear Doctor Clarke. Fancy seeing you again. You won't come in, will you."

"From what little I can remember there is a certain lady I would prefer to keep my arrival from. And she may not be too pleased with you when she finds out you got her instructions wrong."

"Go down to the next level. Rabette will show you where I mean. He did bring you, didn't he?" As the tartan suit flashed past the entrance the Drune's suspicions were confirmed. "Tell him I'm not going to harm him," it called after Walton, but they had gone.

The Drune reopened Pyg's monitor then switched on its surveillance system and buckled a scanner to its narrow waist.

"What happened to my monitor, Drune?" Pyg demanded.

"A fossil must have bitten through a cable somewhere."

"Really?"

"Well, you know what dinosaurs were like."

"Where are you going?"

"To check a fracture in the Lanquitch, the complex below. The Ossiane cladding is so ancient it signals stress failures all the while. The dinosaur will have to wait."

"You are a busy little Drune, aren't you. I hardly know where to find you half the time."

"Well, if you'd like a cauldron of magma dropped in your lap! I doubt if even your immaculate body's temperature control could cope with that."

"Don't be insolent."

"Why? Can you stun me from there?"

"Don't count on there only being one way to punish clever delinquents." The Drune chuckled in defiance. "You'll challenge me once too often," she promised.

"And I thought we were friends."

"Why does the fracture need such immediate attention?"

"As the others live above the old complexes, breakages at these levels aren't going to bother them. I can hardly imagine they would come to your rescue if you sent an SOS."

"Be quick."

"Promise." The Drune bounded off before she could ask any more awkward questions.

The android slid through an ancient buttressed fracture in the hot granite shielding and alighted onto the comparative safety of an uneven staircase. From there it could see any movement in the deserted Lanquitch. As Pyg had no monitors in any old Ossiane city the Drune kept the illumination in them dimly comfortable and the air reasonably sweet. It was one of the agreements it had made with the remaining inhabitants in exchange for their leaving it to pursue its own excavations in peace.

The architecture of Lanquitch was rugged, like the

stubble on the chin of a once handsome fist fighter. The people who had lived here possessed an attitude to existence that made other cities wary about what was imported and exported from and to the place. There was a marked lack of obsidian, or any other material that might furnish a good edge. Unlike the more civilized cities, Lanquitch had been constructed upwards, most of its buildings clinging to vertical walls like semi-detached fungi. An ideal place for experimenting with hang gliders, but not for small Atlantians planning to pounce on dangerous androids. Below the Drune was a very long drop.

On a balcony beneath, the Drune could hear Rabette and Walton whispering. They were alone, so it lowered itself from the overhang and alighted on the floor before them. Its sudden arrival, descending like an elegant spider, even made Walton jump. The creature's silver hair glistened eerily in the half-light and they stepped back into a chamber hewn into the city's shielding.

"Are you alone?" asked the Drune.

Rabette hid behind Walton. "Of course we are. Who else do you think is liable to be down here?"

The Drune advanced on him. "Ghosts perhaps, little brother. Millions and millions of ghosts."

"I did not come here to talk about necromancy," Walton interrupted.

"What did you come here to talk about, Doctor? Post-operative depression?"

"I don't know why you weren't able to close down my mind as that creature told you to but, if it's any consolation, you left me with one hell of a hangover."

"I suppose you realised they would never believe you were carried off by a UFO?"

Walton scowled.

The Drune tried to face Rabette, but he had darted into

the far corner of the room. "Oh little Rabette, what have I done to frighten you?"

"Keep away from me."

"I've no objection to your having a girlfriend."

"Still keep away from me."

"Even if she is buxom enough to smother all three of us."

"Leave him alone you vicious spidery toad," Walton warned.

"Spider? Toad? Oh Doctor, mixed zoological metaphors. Not even I could be both amphibian and arachnid. Though some of them are my best friends." The Drune spread its black gloved hands before Rabette. "Especially spiders, large long legged, wriggling folk who love to drop on little Atlantians."

Rabette broke away in fright to hide in another corner.

The Drune laughed. "What do you make of that Doctor? A race that spent a million years underground finds itself afraid of spiders."

Walton wanted to knock the creature down then and there, but exclaimed instead, "When you've finished indulging your pleasure circuits I think it's about time you gave me some explanations."

"Oh, but there's no fun in that. You'd never believe them anyway. Why don't I introduce you to the Captain and his crew properly? You'd enjoy that."

"They never enjoyed it the last time, and neither did I. I suspect that's another idea you have of a joke." Then Walton roared, "Explanations! Explanations are what I need!"

"Ssh!" the Drune cautioned. "You wouldn't believe the amount of pointing up this city needs. Can't you be angry quietly?"

"I don't know what your game is, but if you believe I am going to stand by while you and your alien friends undermine the fabric of this planet like demented cock-roaches – !" Walton gritted his teeth to prevent any more from escaping.

"Doctor. I do believe I've upset you. And I thought you would at least be pleased that your brain hasn't received the retread I should have given it. After all, it was your birthday wasn't it."

"Pleased!"

"Have you any idea what Pyg would do to me if she found out?"

"Something unspeakable, I hope."

"She actually enjoys tormenting me. Would you believe someone like that? How can anyone get pleasure from making others suffer?"

"You seem to cope quite well."

"I don't count. I'm an android. It's the way I was made."

"It probably isn't its fault really," Rabette added from where he was cringing in a corner.

Walton shook his large head in disbelief. There was something inexplicably compatible about the reluctant companions.

"Look," the Drune said, "why can't we come to some arrangement?"

Walton hesitated. Though irrelevant the proposal might be interesting. "What arrangement?"

The Drune left the trembling Rabette to edge closer to Walton.

"Something that would suit all of us."

"Like?"

"I'll show you the safest way out of here before Pyg finds you, and in return you go back to being a good little astronomer with no hallucinations, curiosity or frightening tales for your lovely little wife."

"How do you know I've got a lovely wife?"

"After three failed marriages you had to get it right eventually."

"You . . ." snarled Walton.

"Now don't get rough." The Drune darted out of range to the entrance. "I'm merely trying to explain how much she would miss you if anything unfortunate happened to you down here."

"You seem sure something unfortunate is going to happen?"

"As much as I enjoy seeing you again Doctor, I really wish you would go. And take Rabette with you."

"You mean take him above ground?"

"Why not?"

"He'd never be accepted."

"You know enough chemistry to give him a complexion. He's been dying to leave the warren for a long while. I'm sure you could find him a good home with plenty of lettuce and tranquilizers."

"I suppose I could." Walton turned to Rabette. "Is this true?" Rabette nodded. "Good grief."

As the Drune watched Walton turn the possibility over in his mind, its eyes glistened mischievously. While it preened itself on consideration of its solution, its guard was dropped. Suddenly something looped past its wide shoulders. With an abrupt crack, its arms were pinned to its body by a strap. Before the Drune could spin round to confront the attackers, a fold of fabric was wrapped round its eyes and pulled tight. Blindly it tried to escape, but a pack of bodies descended from nowhere to push the android off balance and secure its legs. The Drune kicked out and sent the occasional body flying. A powerful hand grasped an ankle and dragged it back into the room.

"Leave it alone now," Walton ordered his accomplices. "You'll only be injured for nothing. Let's not touch it again until we have to. I'm still not sure whether it can activate its defence mechanism."

"Are you sure it has one?" Rabette asked dubiously.

"Are you sure it has one?" mimicked the Drune. "You simpering cheat. Why should I be armed?"

"We're not taking any chances all the same," Walton told it. "I reckon I was right about your eyes. Your co-ordination is dependent on your sight, isn't it?"

"If I have to be such a simple piece of machinery to suit your prejudices, then so be it, Doctor."

"It'll soon be academic anyway, Drune."

"I suppose I'm meant to ask why?"

"We're going to dismantle you."

The Drune sighed. "Oh, messy! Even Auntie Pyg has resisted the temptation of going that far."

"Well we humans do have a vested interest in preventing you from firing that damned missile into the atmosphere."

"Oh what a shame! I thought it was such a good idea."

"By the time we've finished, you will be the scraps of somebody's bad idea."

No longer able to intimidate, the Drune resorted to threats.

"When I escape I'll feed all of you into the nearest magma chamber. It will probably erupt you out, Doctor, and the resulting pollution will blight the countryside for years." The Drune gave an insane laugh. "Are you so sure you want to save your miserable species? Or is it the thought of being a hero? 'Walton the Great – he couldn't explain the Cosmos, so he saved the world'."

"Are you going to shut up?" Walton removed his tie. The Drune's words were putting more fear into the Atlantians than their struggle with it.

"What, Doctor Clarke? You expect me to sign a consent form so you can dissect me?"

Now the Drune's words bit into Walton's conscience.

Swiftly he gagged the android with his tie. "You won't feel a thing, I promise. We'll keep the pieces and hope someone may one day be able to assemble them in a less malevolent way. Failing that, I know a Christmas tree that would benefit from the hair."

18

Akaylia followed the artificial river for some while. She marvelled at the engineering that kept its water from contact with the writhing pressure outside. Just one small fracture and the whole network would be vaporized into a cauldron of steam within a matter of seconds.

Eventually the geologist came to a large lake. The ceiling was low and the water churned turbulently enough to reach it in places. Checking that the capsule was securely sealed, she struck out to investigate the whirlpool at its centre.

The water was being drawn off to feed another source. Helping oxygenate the atmosphere, this system had been flowing and bubbling away for millennia. It would go on doing so until the complex met the mantle and had to succumb to the unevenness of the match. So consumed was she with the spectacle, Akaylia did not notice the angry surge gathering pace to snatch at her. When she did she was already in the eye of the whirlpool, being spun round and round like a descending drill bit.

At the end of her giddy journey the capsule punctured another world of the long-departed Ancients. As it bobbed gently to the surface of a lake, Akaylia immediately saw the reason for Rabette's admiration of the architecture. Nothing like it existed on Earth. It had been erected long before the pyramids and before the Greeks had invented tapering columns and the slavery to construct them. The finely-chiselled fabric of Rosipolees had been made of a stone she could not identify and must have been fashioned with non-sparking tools so their use would not have ignited the oxygen rich atmosphere.

The light was dim and mainly radiated from behind acres of what appeared to be coloured glass. Glittering fountains were scattered everywhere. The translucent fabric was the principal building material so it must have comprised something stronger than sand, soda and potash. Perhaps the hanging walls were stained obsidian, welded together like stained glass. Foundations were probably not necessary here and the buildings on a slowly moving floor hung more securely from supports than they would have done if constructed upon rigid frames.

Akaylia guided the capsule up off the lake. From a higher vantage point, she could see that the only thing to suffer from the desertion of Rosipolees was the foliage. The fossilized skeletons of long extinct trees littered the patios and avenues, though crystal imitations of flowers spangled the stretch of water and were strung like streamers from one roof to another. The latter were somewhat hazardous and she assumed that when the city had been inhabited her mode of transport had been banned. A much greater hazard was created by the spires of a huge crystal edifice at the centre of the city. The building seemed to be covered with frost and stood on several legs, rather like a small palace paddling through a sea of moonlit, multi-coloured waves.

Perhaps she should step out and take a stroll. Colliding with a structure like that would make the destruction of the Crystal Palace seem like a broken windscreen.

Akaylia read the capsule's atmosphere and pressure

gauges. The half-mile thick city shielding and the energy bond holding it rigid were still intact and there was no risk of air poisoning or a sudden crushing pressure to spread her many molecules on the floor. She lowered the capsule to the ground and warily slid back the roof. The air had a strange odour of decay and she could hear the soft pounding of generators converting the planet's energy into usable power.

Clumsily Akaylia toppled out of the capsule. Where to start though? Plazas, bridges, suspended walkways and colonnaded avenues branched in every direction. Whether they were anchored above or below, she decided to give the bridges a miss; she hadn't lost that much weight.

Even the pavements were an artistic delight. They were raised and, made of the same clear material as the walls, were underlit to bathe any walkers in gentle pastel illumination. Akaylia mused over the novel underwear the inhabitants might have worn.

What wonders could be created with unlimited energy! Fountains fed from the lake still played in their canals, although somewhat erratically. Elegant statues of unidentifiable subjects looked down at the unusual intruder with mute interest. A short distance away was the steepled roof of another crystal structure the size of a large tomb. Using her internal compass – her magnetic one had experienced a nervous breakdown long before – she picked her way through the passages and colonnades towards it.

The building gleamed so much it might have been the temple for some computerized god, but the glistening bars and locks spoke more of a prison. Given the elaborate security, she hoped that whatever had escaped from it was well away and not carnivorous. Risking her generous proportions, Akaylia squeezed inside the hollow where the captive had been held. Several silver strands shimmered above her and she plucked them from the seam in the warm crystal. She took out her purse. The hairs were exactly like the tinsel tuft she had snatched from the Drune's mane. It was not only a robotic marvel, but a Houdini as well.

Akaylia pushed herself out and looked around. There were many signs of habitation. Unlike Pompeii, the inhabitants had evacuated Rosipolees rapidly enough to avoid becoming fossils. There were no signs of major accident, so the last disaster to chase out the remaining people had probably been atmospheric . . . unless it had something to do with that prisoner escaping from its crystal cage.

She took a walkway, which led her to a network of connecting balconies. The doors into many of the rooms were hung on frail hinges and were as light as playing cards. Some were emblazoned with devices that indicated either the occupant's trade or state of mind. Akaylia knew that flasks and flowers probably meant a herbalist and scales must mean weights and measures, but the long knotted serpent with a supercilious grin was beyond her. She gingerly pushed the door open and saw a figure, apparently of paper, motionless at its shoe last as though frozen in mid blow with its small hammer. It was surrounded by a disorganized array of heels, soles and tools.

"What an odd sort of display," Akaylia thought to herself and reached out to touch the life-size piece of origami. The meaning of the serpent symbol then became apparent. The paper fell to dust, leaving a very real skeleton beneath it. Hoping the sudden plague virus, which had stricken the cobbler, was extinct, Akaylia beat a hasty retreat down to street level.

Eventually she found a large room that intrigued her. It opened onto the avenue and was cluttered with quite modern equipment. Its owner must have been some sort of polymath and not averse to luxury. Discovering a store of preserved exotic food, Akaylia could not resist sampling it – very generously.

Feeling guilty, she decided to walk off a few ounces. Somewhere in the distance a lift cage darted its way down a shaft and through the city's floor. Akaylia ducked out of sight though she knew it would have been difficult for anybody to see even her from such a distance.

With no sign of the lift's return she continued her stroll through the half-lit panorama in silent appreciation for some while. The sights were so stunning she even forgot to talk to herself. They were beyond rhyming couplets and alliterated adoration. But, strangely enough, her silence was being resented. At first she thought it was only her fancy which heard the soft irregular whistling as she passed each ancient Atlantian statue. But, as the number of statues increased, so did the sound. Walking into a square where three of the creations sat gently throbbing with light and faint murmuring, Akaylia stopped to think.

One of the translucent statues was bowl-like, with a long proboscis and diffused with a comfortable orange light. Its nearest companion, on a low plinth beside it, was more uprightly regal. That had several arms reaching down to touch the pavement and as many colours passing up and down them. The third statue was aloof and intricate with a tall, convoluted design. It was draped elegantly around a large globe balanced on a stalk. As the murmuring rippled on, the light flowing inside it changed hue with each new note.

"My goodness," Akaylia had to gasp aloud. "A scintillating scattering of synchronized statuary." The murmuring increased as though inviting her to say more.

> "Is this the place to discover and see,
> To solve dear old Plato's mystery?"

She could virtually hear the applause of the statues.

"What art in blue, orange, green and crimson,
Has rallied to greet an honorary Atlantian?"

As the murmuring increased they almost became comprehensible.

"Poetry in light and pulsing colours,
Were you designed for courting lovers?
Or perhaps to tell of nature's taming
With smooth cut tunnels and energy framing?"

The statues wanted to burst with words: not necessarily human ones, or in any order. But even Akaylia had to run out of rhymes sooner or later.

"Tell . . . what? What . . . are . . . ?" The largest statue eventually blurted out a gabble of words, as though it had been holding its breath for a million years.

"I am Akaylia," she announced. "Mostly geologist, all woman, and sometimes on a diet."

"I am word analy – "

"Analyzer?"

"Correct."

"A public conversation piece?"

"We make conversation with anyone who desires it."

"And never interrupt?"

"Never."

"You can't be a fellow, then."

"Fellow?"

"Slightly larger, hairier and prone to fits of self esteem."

"Are they related to errand moles?"

Akaylia pondered. "Don't think so. Are they something to do with post wasps?"

"Oh no. There haven't been any of them about for some

time. They have to be locked up because they get very disagreeable when there isn't any mail to deliver."

"The one I met didn't look too pleased when it did have a letter."

"They are so efficient, though. Nothing ever tempts one of them to stop and chat."

"Must be galling."

"Every other unit can offer conversation on some level, though obviously nothing as sophisticated as ours'."

Akaylia took a deep breath. "You mean – everything down here talks?"

"Of course. Some of us will actually listen as well if programmed for it."

"What are you programmed for?"

"Whatever you want to talk about," said the multi-armed statue.

"How about Rosipolees, the evolution of the planet, and the meaning of life in general?"

"Then I am your selection," triumphantly declared the one on the globe. "Though the others may join in if we allow them."

"Well, transparent turmoil of transient translations, let's start with the meaning of life and work our way up."

"Well, I'm generated by impulses fed through the city memory bank and rationalizes . . ."

"Hold it. Let's skip the self-interested bits and go onto the city. How old is it?

"What time is it now?"

Akaylia looked at her stunned solar powered watch. "Ten past twelve."

"That must be a different time base from ours."

"Indubitably. Why does everything down here still work?"

"We were recently overhauled, the power converting generators realigned and stabilized."

"Why?"

"When we are ready, tourists will visit us."

"No kidding?"

"We've got one already, but so far she hasn't come in here."

"Where has she gone then?"

"Burrowed out a hole for herself nearby and stayed there. Antisocial I call it; coming all the way down here and not offering us conversation pieces so much as half a dozen words. Probably got some alien language it would be horrendous to make sense of anyway."

"Mysterious?"

"Can't tell. She keeps herself to herself."

"What is she like?"

"The computer knows, but seldom says much. The creature is a hard hairless specimen. Spindly and severe, like a serpent."

"You suffer from planetary chauvinism."

"Well of course. I'm programmed to. How could we make conversation if we were perfect? No one would dare gossip to us."

"How do I get to meet this adamantine creature then?"

"Oh, I really think you shouldn't try. It would probably frizzle your hair." The conversation piece noticed that nature had got there first. "Well, spoil your appetite, if you set eyes on her. I know we're far from fully functional down here but we can offer you some small entertainments."

"I can blow eighteen flowers into the air and juggle them all at once," agreed the bowl-shaped statue, about to puff the described objects from its body.

"Nobody asked you to join in," admonished its superior and the bowl's radiance dimmed in disappointment. "What about a ride on the lake?"

"That's the way I came in."

"How odd. Is there something wrong with the lift?"

"Oh . . . the lift. Would it go down to your alien visitor by any chance?"

"You are persistent. But if you insist – yes! However, she would know immediately you stepped out of it. If you must be curious, there is another way down."

"Wouldn't her sensors pick me up if I tried it?"

"She doesn't have any in here. Nor does she know about the test shaft that was sunk when Rosipolees was being excavated. The energy barrier is still effective."

"But she would still know when I broke through into her complex?"

"She believes the matrix beneath her control room is impregnable. There is no entrance to it other than her own, so there are no sensors. However . . ."

"Don't start that again. Just tell me how, where and when."

"The city computer is very reluctant."

"Ask her if she can tell me what the alien's doing here?"

"She can't."

"Then how can she be sure it's not something harmful?"

"She can't."

"And what's her prime objective?"

"To protect the planet's life forms."

"So, as this creature isn't a life form of this planet, she doesn't have to protect it."

"I much preferred you when you were spouting rhyming couplets."

"So did I, but cool curiosity is a cruel killer of incandescent creativity."

"Well don't do anything to put the tourists off will you?"

19

The Drune struggled to free itself, tumbling the small Atlantians aside like snowflakes but, with the aid of Walton, it was dragged like a suffocating pike to the bench where it was going to be filleted. As though its circuits knew they were about to be dismembered, they gave the patient such a jolt of energy it almost threw its captors off.

"Quickly, quickly!" bustled Rabette in a trauma of his own. "Pin it down."

Eventually the sheer weight of bodies held its limbs in place long enough for the straps to be fastened. The Drune was at last still. Half expecting it to operate some self-destruct mechanism and vaporize before they could dismantle it, the Atlantians backed off a little and watched.

Somewhere in the labyrinth of Walton's emotions the creature's predicament struck a chord. "Don't do it!" he blurted out.

Rabette was too surprised to speak for a moment. "There's no other way to deactivate it."

"You're a scientist," one of the others agreed. "You of all people must understand that."

"Perhaps there's some way we can control it?" Walton proposed hopefully.

"With these instruments I couldn't even find power units let alone its memory," said Rabette. "The only thing I can do is disconnect its motor tendons and hope we can disassemble it from there."

"What a waste." Walton noticed Rabette's trembling hands. He moved him away from the power switch. "I'll do it."

Guiltily, Rabette approached the Drune and removed one of its gloves to clasp its hand. "I know it's not really that evil. I can sense it sometimes. All the time I've known it, it's never harmed me." He combed its ruff back with his fingers. "I think I'll miss it."

One of his companions became annoyed that he had chosen that moment to get sentimental over the android. "It's a machine, Rabette."

"It's a friend, a tormentor, a confidant, an enemy – ." Then Rabette withdrew his hand in horror. He had never touched the Drune's skin before; it had never allowed anyone to do so.

Walton was poised to throw the switch that would rupture every connection in its body.

"No! Wait!" screamed Rabette.

Walton was startled by the sudden outburst. "What the . . ."

"Come here. Feel its skin." Rabette removed its blindfold.

Hesitantly Walton's large hand hovered over the hair-free centre of the Drune's face then lowered itself onto its nose and cheeks. He was as amazed at the discovery as Rabette. He rummaged in his pocket for a penknife.

"Don't hurt it," whispered Rabette.

"Not much."

Walton pushed back the Drune's sleeve and made a nick in its wrist with the sharp blade. A small trickle of blood issued from the wound. A circle of apprehensive white faces looked down in wonder.

"But it can't be alive," murmured Rabette. "The skin's so grey."

"Mine's beige, yours is milk white. Many animals have grey skin; it's not unusual. In this case it's the animal that is unlikely," explained Walton.

"But what sort of animal is it?"

"If it's not from a species of elf or hobgoblin, it can't be of this planet."

"How can we be sure it isn't some sophisticated alien machine? Blood can be counterfeited."

"Undress it. I know enough about biology to make an informed guess."

Rabette hesitated. "It won't like it."

"Why should it? It's not its birthday."

Intimidated by their discovery the Atlantians backed away. They realised they had almost been parties to murder.

Walton efficiently unfastened the Drune's tunic without releasing the straps round its neck and waist. Even though he was saving its life, the Drune was far from enthusiastic about his heavy hands feeling out pulses and reflexes with casualty ward competence. It recoiled at every prod and pressure and showed definite signs of wishing to throttle its doctor.

The beardless Atlantians were transfixed at the sight of the torso covered with silver hair. Walton had to admit he was a little bewildered as well. Even if he hadn't been convinced after that, a sizable scar under the fine fur proved its mortality beyond any doubt.

Walton angrily cut off the Drune's gag, taking a tuft of its hair as he did so. "Why didn't you tell us? We could have killed you."

The Drune scowled. "I wasn't aware I gave the impression I wanted you to."

"What the devil are you for pity's sake?"

"Aluminium poisoning."

Walton quickly withdrew his hand before the sarcasm registered. "You nearly ended up as a set of saucepans."

Timidly, Rabette reached out and gently ruffled the fur on the neuter's body. "Don't torment it."

Unaware that he was, and satisfied about the Drune's living biology, Walton backed away.

"How strange," pondered Rabette. "How strange! What can we do with you?"

"Try fastening my tunic and finding something to mollify that hyperactive gorilla."

Rabette stopped pawing the Drune and carefully did up its tunic, teasing out its ruff from the high collar as he did so. "What do we do now?"

"We still need to know how to immobilize that infernal device it made," Walton reminded Rabette.

"But it'll never tell us that."

"Not if we ask it nicely. I wasn't thinking of being polite though." The Drune's expression clouded as the gist of the suggestion became apparent. "Now we know it isn't a machine. All flesh and blood can feel pain."

Unfortunately his bluff convinced Rabette as effectively as it had the Drune.

"No!" Rabette placed himself in absurd interposition between Walton and the prisoner. "You're not torturing it. I don't care what it's done."

The Drune's expression relaxed into mocking amusement. Walton lifted Rabette from the ground and gave him a vigorous shake. "I should let my second wife's poodles have you for dinner."

"There's no need to be violent," Rabette protested bravely, not entirely sure what manner of ferocious beast a poodle was.

Walton tossed Rabette aside and turned on the Drune. "And there's no reason for you to laugh. I still have a debt to settle. Start finding things funny now and it could be redeemed as several instalments on the end of my fist. Don't believe your colossal intellect is going to help you either. I'm the one with the upper hand now."

The Drune sneered. "That's the trouble with too much education, it goes straight to the ego. You were never emotionally equipped to be a thug and too blunted at the corners to engage in fluid reasoning."

A flush of rage rose under Walton's collar. "What I do know I make use of by trying to pass it on to others. For all your genius you're about as much use as a plague virus and twice as deadly."

"Only double the potency Doctor? I would have thought I was at least as mischievous as a class of your deluded students by the time you'd finished educating them."

The astronomer seized a handful of the Drune's hair in half a mind to twist its head off. "Someone with your intelligence should be aware of what it's doing."

The Drune gave a mortal wince. "Oh but I am, and I'm sure if you had that bolt in your neck loosened, the improved flow of blood to your brain would open up a few perceptive cells as well. Please don't pull my hair like that, it's giving me a terrible headache." Walton increased his grip to see if it would turn off the creature's tongue. "Haven't you any influence over this aggressive monument to human culture, little brother?"

Rabette gingerly tugged its tormentor's hand away and massaged the Drune's scalp. He told Walton, "It's only being spiteful because we've upset it. Don't pay any attention."

"Even if I did tell you how to disengage the missile, I doubt if you could work out the right switches to push," sighed the Drune.

"You might even push the wrong ones," Rabette added unhelpfully.

"Why don't you go and find some rope?"

Rabette was apprehensive. "What for?"

"We'll either have to tie it up or leave it here."

"But for how long?"

"How long do you think it'll take us to find the missile?" Walton threatened the Drune.

"Assuming my dumb little friend is unable to remember the way there – forever."

"Well?" Walton asked Rabette.

Rabette plucked at the Drune's ruff in irritation and guilt.

"All right," Walton decided. "The Drune stays here. It may be comfortable now, but it's surprising how hard surfaces become after several hours. It'll have no food or water either." He beckoned to the more reliable Atlantians. "Make sure it's secure. Tighten the straps just in case." Then he grasped Rabette's arm. "And we shall take a grand tour to jog your memory."

20

Following the directions of the conversation pieces, Akaylia found Rosipolees' ancient test shaft. It was capped by a drab looking building that sat like a giant turtle over a precious egg. As there was no entrance it could have been sealing off a build-up of pressure. Taking a meter from the capsule, she checked its density. It was very thick.

A tub-shaped machine on independently driven wheels rolled up to meet her. Through the clear casing Akaylia could see the sparking of its circuits as they perpetually checked each component. At each movement the machine looked as though it was about to burst into flames, and she was sure that irregular clicking noise had more to do with its disposition than operational function.

"What kept you?" she asked.

"I was in store," the mechanic explained grumpily. "And the other equipment you asked for is going to take a good deal longer."

"Not to worry. It's all in a good cause."

"That's what the city computer told me. What did you say to convince her?"

"I'll explain it all later, bowl of baleful benevolence. How about giving me a hand with the lid?"

"I don't have a hand."

"I meant, can you open it for me, parsnip pot?"

"There's no need to be personal."

"Touchy little mobile mind, aren't you."

"I was not programmed as a conversation piece. I'm a mechanic."

"So open the lid, swivel brain."

"Oh all right. But stand well back. Even though the molecular bonding should be stable, the atmosphere must be very compressed after all this while."

Akaylia obeyed. She could see the mechanic activating several different codes in its body, and then it suddenly flipped a huge bolt of energy at the dome. The plasma quivered a little before spreading itself over the shell, like melting gelatin. With a painful cracking and creaking, the centre of the dome started to lift. A release of foul-smelling atmosphere came out of the shaft with such violence the lid was hurled back and fell from its hinges.

"Oh," cursed the mechanic. "Why did they have to build everything so well?"

Akaylia held her breath. The alien's equipment must have registered the impact.

"Can you send out another signal to confuse the matrix scanners?"

"No problem." The mechanic trundled off towards a row of solid looking buildings. With dispassionate precision it shot out a beam, which dismantled the first it came to. After a slight groan the avenue collapsed like a pack of cards. "Floor movement. Brings down buildings all the time."

"Vandal."

"Better than bringing the aliens up here."

"True."

Akaylia and the mechanic waited to make sure no investigation was going to be launched from below. The only objects to show curiosity were several mobile conversation pieces, an errand mole and one or two dismayed cleansing units. Akaylia sensed they were berating the mechanic but, whatever they were saying, it showed no signs of apology.

"Right," Akaylia announced. "Time we started work."

"If you are going into that shaft, make sure the capsule's pressurized. I don't know what's happened down there after all this while."

"Couldn't be any leaks could there?"

"Not until you start cutting a tunnel to the other complex."

"But the computer was sure the shield's bonding was safe enough to burrow through."

"So she's a mathematician and I'm a mechanic. As the alien managed to build both her matrix and control inside the shield she must be right, I suppose."

"How did the alien manage to cut through the energy bond holding the rock solid?"

"Strong teeth, no doubt."

"So what does a filly with a face full of fillings do?"

"Wait for the appropriate equipment, as you were told."

"All right peevish package. In the meantime I'll take a look around. Oh – and thanks."

The lights in the mechanic blinked a bad tempered farewell before it trundled off, sparking and clicking away to itself.

Akaylia returned to the capsule and pressurized it as instructed. Switching on all its floodlights she gently lowered it into what must have been the deepest hole in the planet. It was also the least immaculate. Being an experimental bore, the walls were irregular and blotched. There were prominences where the engineers had tried to brighten it up with a little statuary, but Akaylia preferred not to dwell on what they might have depicted. The walls also acted like a resonating chamber and picked up strange noises from beneath the planet's crust. They were like the yawns of a ghostly giant about to wake and push a mighty fist through the thin moho. For a moment the geologist hesitated. She knew she was balancing on a tightrope which divided human experience from cosmic reality; the Universe where mere mortal life forms meant nothing on the ladder to Galactic evolution.

With some difficulty Akaylia shook off reality and used Rabette's instruments to pinpoint the alien's excavations. Two large cavities, one on top of the other, sat snugly in the protection of the shielding. The city computer had not misled her. It would be possible to bore through to the lower chamber's wall. To prevent herself or the excavating equipment from falling the rest of the way down the shaft, she lowered a safety bridge from the belly of the capsule and bolted it across the hole into the opposing walls. Then she went back up to await the arrival of her next mechanical ally.

The longer Akaylia waited the more she wondered how the heavy plant needed to do the job would fit into the shaft. She had convinced herself it was impossible by the time a small box of lights hovered up to her. Thinking it was a messenger to say that the heavy equipment was going on a diet, at first she paid little attention to it. Then it skittered about as though on elastic, trying to attract her attention.

It coughed politely and apologised. "Sorry about the delay. The hovering facilities were a little wonky." It was only then that she realised that this was the heavy plant.

"But how could you manage to drill a hole wide enough for me to get through?"

"Oh, I'm not a drill," it explained. "I'm an energy unbonder."

"A what?"

"I simply unbind the energy bond holding the molecules steady and the rock trickles away."

"Oh, of course." Akaylia wondered how she could have overlooked such an elegant explanation. Perhaps she was getting so used to the bizarre that simplicity seemed absurd. "Shall we go?"

"No. I'll go. You wait here."

"But . . ."

"When rock melts so do many other things it comes into contact with, even the occasional capsule. And, as I notice you have no hovering facilities, all you need do is indicate the position of the bore."

"I marked everything up, but stop a centimetre short of the matrix. We don't know how often the alien sits in her parlour."

"Trust me." The energy unbonder floated over the shaft. "Be back in no time."

As daintily as a jet-propelled butterfly, the machine faintly thrummed its way down until Akaylia lost sight of it. A soft sizzling sound echoed upwards, soon accompanied by the odd gurglings and gluggings resembling a fast flowing river of treacle.

After a few moments the molecular acrobatics were complete and the unbonder thrummed its way back up to announce, "I've made a spyhole for your height."

"Wonderful," Akaylia congratulated it. "How do I break through when the coast is clear?"

"Just push against the wall. A machine your size will have no problem. It's only a centimetre thick, as instructed, and molecularly weakened."

Not flattered that the apparatus had been treating her with such courtesy because it thought she was one of its kin, Akaylia thanked it as kindly as she could and returned to the capsule.

Sure enough, a long tunnel wide enough to let her comfortably pass had been neatly melted through the shielding. The energy unbonder had even tailored it to match her vital statistics, no doubt under the impression that, as she was a machine, her body was not very flexible.

Through the spyhole at the other end of the tunnel Akaylia could see that the interior of the matrix was bathed in an unnecessarily bright light, as though it was perpetually in use. But when she took in more of the large room there was nothing but bland boxes. Well practised in most forms of demolition, these made the geologist pause for thought. How was she going to get inside them to switch anything off? She knew she had to do it, since the systems they contained must have been controlling the minds of the "Atlantian" engineers after the aliens had disposed of the rest of their population. It was probably only a matter of time before they started to sort out life on the Earth's surface as well.

Carefully Akaylia pushed at the wall with the heel of her hand and made the spyhole larger. No sirens wailed and no gongs clattered. She set to work with the rest of her anatomy and was soon able to enter an unnerving prospect. For a moment she was at a loss what to do. There must have been a local scanner of some sort. She froze when she saw a small, closed eye-like lens just above her head. Fortunately it never blinked, so it had to be asleep. Not sure how long that happy situation would last, Akaylia returned to the capsule, sent a message to the grumpy mechanic, then dispatched the capsule back up on automatic to collect it.

"Kill that," she ordered as soon as the mechanic arrived.

Without its usual bleep of irritation the mechanic sent out a shaft of pink light and the scanner's eye sizzled.

"Won't that raise an alarm?"

"It was on a loop. Checks for 30 minutes, sleeps for 30 minutes."

"Why?"

"Probably gets tired easily."

Akaylia gave up and pointed to the large bland cubes housing the alien's equipment. "What are they doing?"

The mechanic blinked its lights in concentration for a few seconds. "Sending out signals."

"What signals?"

"You should know. They're nearer to your brain wave patterns than mine."

"Cubes sending out brain wave pattern signals. I see!" Akaylia smiled mischievously. "I think it's about time Atlantis was given a headache."

21

Walton made Rabette search every lower tunnel and cavern built by the Atlantians until he felt as though the top of his head had been flattened by the pressure, but the Drune proved to have been a remarkable excavator. Its complex was hidden far beneath theirs. To make things worse, Rabette fancied that his descent with the Drune had started under a concealing overhang and there were plenty of those in that sector. If only the route map had not been erased when he had reached home! The Drune had obviously intended that Rabette should not make a return visit.

Rabette insisted on turning the capsule back. Though he dare not admit it, he was hoping the Drune had somehow managed to escape. But the idea had crossed Walton's mind as well.

"Where would the Drune go if we released it?"

"I don't know." Rabette held his breath for fear of saying something to divert his train of thought.

"It's too sharp to lead us back to the missile of course."

"Of course."

"It might head straight to its mistress. It must be in quite a state by now and wouldn't be able to get very far on foot.

Assuming it couldn't launch the missile without her authorization it would have to report in first."

"Shall I release it?"

Walton pondered. "Perhaps not. It would know it was being followed."

"But we can't leave it where it is. There's no point if it can't be persuaded to talk."

"I don't trust it."

"It doesn't expect us to. It's our only chance."

Walton paused to wonder at Rabette's badly concealed enthusiasm. "Why are you so fond of the abominable creature?"

"I don't know. I can't explain it. I sometimes have this feeling that everything is wrong."

"Wrong?"

"As though reality has been slewed to one side and we've fallen through the crack."

Walton was relieved to know that his senses weren't the only ones playing the giddy goat. "Must be connected to something the alien is doing. I wish I could remember what she told me."

"No, this is something different. The Drune itself doesn't scare me, only the thought of it. It's confusing to find out that it's a living being after all. I've never had to think about it being harmed before."

"Why worry about it being harmed now?"

"I wish I knew. There's something I feel I should remember, like a frightening dream. Crazy Akaylia could probably explain it. I wish I knew where she was." Then Rabette pleaded. "Tell me I can let the Drune go. It could die if we leave it there much longer. Those straps must be stopping its circulation."

"All right. We'll hide the capsules and make it walk. Several of us will station ourselves in all the routes out so it won't see anyone following it. At least one of us must be able to keep track of it." Walton added in the tone of mild threat, "Satisfied?"

"I promise I won't mess everything up."

That was a welcome assurance for Walton. He suspected that Rabette's competence in some things exceeded his common sense in most others and his brain was merely a stand-by for when his emotions seized up.

As the Drune was fastened down securely, the squeamish Atlantians had left it to endure its stubborn resolve in throbbing peace, only calling every hour to see if it had been shaken. Its skin may not have been plastic after all, but it had a will of iron.

By the time Walton and Rabette returned, the Drune was unpleasantly aware of how hard its bed had become. Every muscle, sinew and joint felt as though it was about to burst and its head pounded painfully on whichever side touched the bench. Although an Atlantian had released the strap round its neck the swelling throughout its body made the other fastenings cut into its flesh all the more.

Seeing the miserable state it was in, Walton had to admit he hated himself for being responsible. Even if he hadn't agreed to let Rabette release it he would have probably done so himself, but everything had to look convincing.

"Well?" growled Walton. "You've had time to think."

"Yes." The Drune somehow smiled, "and I still think you're an egotistical slob, though now I can phrase it in a hundred different ways."

At the sound of the voice, although parched, Walton's sympathy took a sudden battering. He half-heartedly raised his fist, but Rabette more enthusiastically held his arm back. The Drune still seemed amused at their double act. Its smirk of contempt was hardly asking for sympathy.

"Leave it alone," Rabette said with unexpected firmness and, with unusual compliance, Walton turned, banged his skull on the lintel, then stalked out of the chamber.

Rabette filled a phial with water and lifted the Drune's head to pour the fluid down its throat. There was no need to ask how thirsty it was.

"Thank you little brother," it gasped. "I hope that wasn't bribery?"

Rabette was irritated. He could see that the Drune wasn't going to give him the ghost of an excuse to release it.

"Are you comfortable?" he asked.

"Of course I'm not comfortable. I'm only hoping insensibility comes before the final agony."

"I'm sorry."

The Drune chuckled. "Are you?"

"I would like to release you."

"Do you want me to ask you?"

"No . . . *no!*"

"Plead with you?"

Rabette walked away. He was out of his depth already.

"I'm so dangerous, though, am I not?"

"Why did you let us believe you were an android?"

"I wish I could explain."

"Try."

"I wish I could make you understand but your mind is too bound up in a fantasy."

"That monster you work for is real. Walton remembered it as well. You never managed to brainwash him you know."

"That was due to the thickness of his skull, not my incompetence."

"Why were you going to destroy the Earth's surface with that missile?"

"Would you believe me if I said that I wasn't?"

"No."

"Then perhaps I hate everyone. Perhaps it's the only way I can express it."

"But why should you hate them so much?"

"Until Pyg, self expression for Drunes was very limited and insanity was out of the question. Everyone else cured their own madness by going for long holidays in the lower levels. Drunes were cured by the threat of liquidation."

"Who are you talking about?"

"Everyone."

Rabette put the Drune's allegations down to delirium, but knew he had to find the thread that would unravel its distrust. "Who could have treated you so terribly, you would ally yourself with an alien?"

"Not just one little brother – not just one."

"Do you hate me?"

The Drune was silent for some while. It eventually asked, "Come here little brother."

Rabette gazed down into the Drune's purple eyes. How could he have looked into their hypnotizing depths before and not known the creature was mortal? They glittered with life and resentment. Rabette found himself pondering on the nature of the Drune. What was it? Alien or Earthly aberration? If it had fallen off someone's Christmas tree it would have made world headlines. But then, it seemed to be more likely the product of some government's weapon research. Given its practical knowledge of nuclear missiles and apparent indestructibility, some frantic agents might have been combing the planet's surface for it.

"What happened to you?" Rabette could no longer resist asking.

"Happened?"

"You must have been in some sort of experiment to look like that?"

"I was chrome-plated at a very early age."

"Tell me?"

"Brush the hair from my eyes."

Gently Rabette pushed the damp strands away. The touch of the Drune's warm skin kindled even more confusion.

"If I promise to let the missile remain on its launch pad will you release me?"

"Why should I believe you?"

"Because you want to. Everyone will swear a lie is the truth if the alternative is too threatening. Only I'm not lying to you. Trust me."

"Why?"

"For a million reasons I cannot explain."

"Tell me one then?"

"I will probably die if your diplomaed diplodocus insists on leaving me here."

"Walton wouldn't let that happen. We're all likely to die if we let you go."

"What could I get up to in my condition?"

Rabette unfastened the Drune's tunic and efficiently examined it. It lay patiently still while awaiting his verdict.

"Well, am I so athletically dangerous?"

"You're swelling badly. There might be blood clots forming."

"I do have blood little brother," the Drune reminded him. Rabette hesitated, but it could see he was weakening. "Have I ever done anything to harm you before?"

"No," he admitted reluctantly.

"I swear I'll do nothing to harm anyone now. Especially not you, perplexed pixie."

"You have tormented me though," Rabette reminded it.

"I probably will again, but I will never harm you."

Rabette was convinced by its words and it frightened him. His fingers tugged the straps away from their fastenings. The Drune let him lift it into a sitting position and massage the feeling back into its limbs. Slowly it tried to move off the bench but its legs crumpled once they took its weight. If it were unable to walk, Walton's plan would be useless. Rabette left it on the floor and dashed into the medical chamber to find a stimulant. When he returned, the Drune had gone.

He had not given the agreed signal and knew the others wouldn't be in position. Rabette sped after it. It was not difficult to tell which direction it had taken. An Atlantian, wearing an expression of surprise and annoyance, was picking herself up from the floor of a passage. So, still clutching the stimulant, he pursued the Drune.

Managing to follow the Drune's route by snatching glimpses of its glinting hair and black tunic Rabette wondered at its speed considering the state it must have been in.

Eventually the tunnels of the Atlantians came to an end and those of the alien began. A sliding slab of granite concealed the entrance. The others would have never guessed their whereabouts. Should he go in, or report back?

Taking his chance, Rabette eased his small body past the seal before it rumbled shut. Then he came to a lift shaft. There were at least half a dozen cages ready to descend to the city of Rosipolees. It had been sealed off centuries before but the Drune and the aliens must have included it in their complex. The Drune was already going down. Rabette waited a safe length of time, then followed it in another cage.

After passing through the ancient city, the Drune stumbled out before it could notice Rabette following. He darted into the passage after it. Rabette slackened his pace as the walls widened. There was an imposing shutter ahead. It opened to let the Drune pass. In the pool of light on the other side he saw it crumple into a heap. Then he did the very thing he had promised Walton he would not do. He messed things up.

Not knowing what demented reflex action inspired him, Rabette dashed through the shutters to the Drune. Kneeling beside it he administered the stimulant. Immediately the

Drune looked up in wide-eyed amazement. It raised its hand to indicate the shutter as the shutter itself slammed shut. The pool of light widened to fill the interior of a large chamber. Rabette was unable to take it all in at once and, after seeing what was seated on the dais above them, the rest of the scenery hardly mattered.

"Well, well," Pyg whirred in sinister satisfaction, "A white rabbit."

It was the creature Rabette had seen staring out at him from the globe.

22

"How – gone?" demanded Walton as he hurtled back into the medical station.

"It tricked us, but I know which way they went," said the Atlantian who had been bowled over. "Follow me."

Despite the urgency of the situation the Drune's black glove, lying on the bench, caught Walton's attention. In its empty fingers was the stem of a long dead flower. The petals were well preserved and as Walton was about to identify them an urgent voice called, "Come on or we'll lose them." The astronomer retracted his mental tentacles and dashed after the others.

Their capsules were able to make good time down the route Rabette had taken. But, although they followed it for miles, covering any side passages, there was no trace of Rabette or the Drune.

Walton's apprehension grew. "We should have caught up with them ages ago."

"I know," agreed Anniya. "We've been out of our own sector for some while. The Drune must have had a hidden shutter somewhere."

"Any chance of finding it?"

"Not very likely. It would have taken care to have shielded it against our scanners."

"But why did the idiot have to follow it by himself? He knows how dangerous it is."

Anniya shook her head. "Rabette thinks well of everything. He doesn't understand why one creature should harm another without reason. He was probably afraid we might harm the Drune if we caught it first."

"Now it's probably caught him."

"He can look after himself."

"I'll throttle that creature with my bare hands if it has harmed him."

Anniya sat back to ponder on the six-passage junction ahead. "Do you think you could remember the way it took to that alien's complex?"

"If you could show me the way I came in."

"It could be dangerous, but there's nothing else for it. I'll call the others back."

"No, wait." Walton suddenly felt the weight of middle-aged absent-mindedness. "It will take too long. The Drune could have killed Rabette and launched that missile before I could work it out. Since that creature tampered with my memory it feels like a colander, and I keep getting the weird feeling that nothing down here is right."

Anniya gave him a blank look to avoid revealing what she was really thinking. "Perhaps these depths disagree with you?" she suggested, though suspecting few things would dare disagree with Walton, even reality. "Perhaps we should try and find the missile instead?"

"Rabette said it was very deep."

"We have the equipment to find such a cavity. The only problem is that there are many cavities in the crust. Even with all of us taking soundings we could search forever."

"Surely you have the plans of the chambers your ancestors excavated?"

"Yes, but not the ones the planet has made. Though we might be able to detect their different atmospheres and save time that way."

"Let's get on with it then."

Fitted with transmitters and receivers, the Atlantian capsules spread out through the tunnels in a complex grid. At short and regular intervals signals were pulsed down at an angle to the planet's mantle and caught in the opposing craft's antenna. Backwards and forwards, higher and lower, they buzzed until their fruitless search persuaded Anniya to admit to Walton, "The Drune must have managed to screen that as well. It has to be nearer the mantle than we think."

"Damn," Walton cursed. "If only I could remember enough to describe that city to you."

"There are so many deserted cities."

Walton took the faded flower from his wallet. "What is this?"

Anniya carefully looked the fragile specimen over.

"Where did you get it?"

Walton shrugged. "It looked as though the Drune had left it for Rabette to find. Probably didn't think he would give chase."

"That is odd," said Anniya, becoming thoughtful, "but it makes me think I should remember something."

"I only hope that whatever it is, it isn't important."

"Perhaps it means that the Drune is fond enough of Rabette not to harm him?"

"Let's hope so."

23

"Come here little Rabette," Pyg cooed.

Although the sight of her was terrifying and the voice chillingly alien, something in her relaxed manner gave Rabette confidence. He went to the dais.

"Why were you so anxious to help that horrible Drune? It is an unspeakably wicked creature."

"I know, but it was damaged."

"And you thought you would repair it for me?"

Because Pyg also appeared to be under the impression that her lackey was an android, Rabette was confused. He turned back to look at the expressionless Drune kneeling on the floor. There was going to be no prompt from that direction.

"I think you are really fond of the Drune," she whirred.

Rabette looked up in protest.

"I've watched you. How you touch its hair when it isn't looking. It fascinates you doesn't it?"

"It's never harmed me. It's not evil."

"No?" laughed Pyg. "What blind devotion, little one."

Rabette was suddenly aware of the absurdity in this chilling situation. He would probably have been less confused if the fearful alien had been slimily green, breathed smoke and communicated by waving its fins. Pyg's mother-of-pearl elegance and towering presence would have been more believable on some of the ancient friezes Atlantians had found in early excavations.

"Who are you anyway?" he demanded angrily.

"Such spirit as well. What shall we do with this creature, Drune?"

The Drune rose wearily. "I'll take Rabette back up and give him something to kill the memory of us."

"No!" protested Rabette.

"It will not hurt you, little brother. There are worse things we could do."

Rabette was silent. Some irrationally annoying intuition was telling him to trust the creature. His logic had long since ceased to function.

"Now you can stroke its hair," Pyg told Rabette.

The Drune stepped back. "No."

"What has happened to you, Drune?"

"Nothing."

"We captured it," declared Rabette. "We were going to dismantle it but changed our minds."

"Why would the Atlantians want to do a thing like that?"

"They're frightened of me," the Drune said quickly. "Their ancestors warned them what would happen if I were released."

Rabette didn't know why, but he suddenly checked himself from contradicting the Drune.

"Why should you bother them?"

"They think I interfere. But while I'm annoying them I am leaving your hot headed, cold blooded crew alone, am I not?"

Pyg resisted the temptation to admonish its sarcasm. She had already thought up a more effective cure for it. "Fetch me my main monitor, Drune."

The Drune leapt onto the dais and pushed out a large panel, which slotted into place beside Pyg's throne.

"Such a cumbersome piece of equipment," Pyg told Rabette who was watching in apprehension. "But it does so much. Look!" She pushed a couple of buttons and on the opposite side of the chamber the wall slid away. "My prison."

Rabette retreated at the sight of the totally bare cavity.

"It's all right little one, not for you. In there I can suspend any creature indefinitely. It's like a life support system without the mess. The body functions are reduced to practically nothing, but the brain remains active. That's how to monitor mortals; make them give you their thoughts. I collect the thoughts of humans – didn't you know?"

"What humans?"

"All the humans on this planet little one. We have been experimenting with them. Even you." She pressed another button causing a screen to appear from nowhere on the opposite wall. It was filled with rows of tumbling symbols. They rained by so fast Rabette was unable to take them in. "That is our input."

"But why? Curiosity can't be the only reason to travel light years and invade a planet."

Pyg hesitated. For the first time she wasn't totally sure herself. She had never met anyone with Rabette's guileless way of putting a question.

"The Ealinans love the idea of control," explained the Drune. "They originally controlled the ecology of this planet until it had had enough of them, then they controlled the output of their next sun until it threatened to burn itself out, and now, finally, they have been reduced to controlling the minds of mere mortals like you."

Pyg was quiet for a moment. "How do you know so much about the Ealinans?" she asked. "Have you been spying on the ship's memory?"

The Drune refused to apologize. "So what?"

Pyg scratched the palm of her hand. Rabette watched in curiosity as the Drune flinched.

"When I eventually have that memory of yours, I will crush it like ripe fruit until all those insolent thoughts are bled away. Then I will plug your dried out brain into my computer so everything you know will be Ealinan."

"Ripe fruit," mocked the Drune. "I'd have thought your species would have been more adept with bloated maggots."

"Shut up!" Rabette whimpered in terror.

"Your little friend has made use of his limited education."

"He's nothing more than a harmless gnat."

"Obviously."

"Why not let him go? Time is getting short."

"What will you do with us when you've finished?" asked Rabette.

"Nothing, nothing at all," said Pyg. "We have all the data we need. Shall we leave tomorrow? I can see you would be happy if we did." There was a disbelieving silence. "Our ship is in countdown. The scout craft are safely stowed. Would you like to come with us?"

"No!"

"The Drune says it will."

Rabette looked at the Drune with a mixture of betrayal and puzzlement.

"He would never survive the voyage," the Drune reminded her. "The cryogenic chamber could not be adapted for his biology."

"No, of course not." Pyg pressed another switch. A large cylinder rotated up through the floor and its door slid open. "The temperature range is far too low for his delicate biology. So very, very low."

"He would die in seconds."

"Clever Drune. I sometimes wonder what I would have

done without you. You had better prepare to board, or can you survive without your memory?"

"I'll take Rabette and give the drug first."

"It isn't necessary."

"I must go back to the lab and seal the complex anyway."

"Is there any need?"

"But he can't stay down here or come with us."

"I didn't have either in mind, faithful Drune. You may leave as soon as you've obeyed me." The whirring remained ominously in her throat after she had spoken.

"Why shouldn't I obey you?"

"I don't know, but I do have this feeling that if I were to let you go now . . ."

"I've always obeyed you."

"I know. But just one more order before we leave."

"All right, I'll do it," insisted the Drune. "What is it?"

Pyg's fingers wandered idly over the monitor controls. "Put your little friend in the cryogenic chamber please."

The Drune was silent for a moment.

"But he's harmless," it laughed.

"I did say 'please' and it will save time. If you must go back to your lab, or collect your memory – or do anything else – you will not have time to deal with him."

The Drune knew Pyg well enough to realize she wasn't joking. It dare not hesitate. It sprang from the dais and seized the terrified Rabette.

Rabette was horrified and indignant. "What are you doing? You can't kill me. I saved your life."

The Drune stopped.

"Do it," Pyg whirred threateningly. "That will make it the second time it's saved your life."

The Drune pulled Rabette to the cryogenic chamber and strapped him to the chair inside.

Some self-deception may have been telling both of them that Pyg was only doing it to frighten because they fell silent like mechanical mice waiting for the turn of a key. But as they looked at each other, their lives and illusions flashed before them.

"Well, come away now, Drune."

As if its key had been given a half turn it stepped back three paces.

Pyg punched the button that closed the door. "Come here, Drune." It obeyed and she pointed to the control that would activate the chamber. "Press that."

"It's set to freeze." The Drune now realised she wasn't bluffing and wished it had been frightened enough to do something when it had the chance. It could have reached inside to the chamber's controls and overridden the thermostat, or set the door to open as it descended into the matrix.

"Do you want to depart this planet without your memory? If you defy me you will not leave this control until the ship takes off. Do you want to spend eternity embedded in its computer? It may contain the knowledge to sail a ship across this galaxy but after the first few light years its conversation can become very boring. If your little friend doesn't die now, the comet will get him later."

"You do it."

"Machines should not develop moral outrage when their survival depends on dispassionate action." Pyg's eyes gleamed with a fierceness, which drained her prey of the insolence to answer. "Do it!" she snarled.

The Drune pressed the button. A puff of white mist was pushed from the test vent to indicate it was working, then the cylinder started to rotate and slowly descend to the matrix below.

"Now you may go."

She opened the chamber shutter. Without a word, the Drune turned and walked out.

Instead of going to the lift cages, it used an ancient

escalator to Rosipolees. Despite the fact the stairs were juddering through lack of rational maintenance, the Drune never moved until it was precipitated onto a badly lit pathway. Walking steadily, as though afraid its limbs would buckle if it tried to run, it passed a building like a monstrous honeycomb. From nowhere a post wasp stopped dead before the Drune and defied it not to take the letter it offered. The Drune ignored the post wasp and kept on walking until it came to a small capsule bay.

The wasp was furious. If all its customers acted as though they were being offered subpoenas, its swarm would soon be out of business. Dispassionately the Drune checked the flight worthiness of a vehicle, then climbed in. Before it could take off, the wasp grasped the letter in its mandibles and held it against the driver's window like a psychotic traffic warden. The Drune noted who it was from, but still ignored it. The wasp tenaciously kept pace with the capsule as it ascended and hovered over the lake, thrumming all of its legs on the roof and whirring insanely.

Suddenly the capsule plunged into the water and disappeared, leaving the wasp to dart this way and that to find a route after it. Water was not its element. It would have shorted out its machinery as surely as it would have destroyed the mail. Its mandibles rattled so much in annoyance they serrated the sides of the envelope before its circuits were resigned to replacing it in its satchel. Then, like a bullet, the post wasp shot to the head of the shaft Akaylia had uncovered, hovered for a few seconds, then plummeted straight down it.

"Oh dear," one of the statues by the lake whispered confidentially to its neighbour perched on a bridge. "I can see we're going to have trouble with the Ossianes when they come back."

The other conversation piece turned its spiralling neck to

make sure the post wasp had gone. "Not like the grey creature. It's never behaved that way before. I blame that wasp myself. Revolting machines. Difficult to tell if they want to deliver a letter or sting you to death."

"Errand mole wouldn't have been quick enough. They're steady, I know, but useless for express deliveries. I heard that the main computer is going to do something about their wheels and eyesight."

"How did you know?"

The statue by the lake stretched to its full height of three and a half feet. "I have a relative up there."

"You mean you were twinned?"

"Yes. They thought my design so perfect I was duplicated. My twin can contact me through our city computer and me through his because they can't tell the difference between our signals."

The bridge statue flushed a little in envy and tried to think of some way to top the revelation as it dipped a tentacle in the water to cool its body fluid. "Wonder what was inside that letter?"

There was a thoughtful hum from the lakeside. "Bet it was important."

"Probably something to do with the grey creature killing a white one."

There was a long gasp of indignation. "How did you know that?"

"I'm listening to the city computer. She's talking to the mechanic that went down the shaft."

"What about?"

"How to get into boxes and what to do when they're open. There's something about a body as well."

"Well I never! A murder! In all my years I've never had a real murder to gossip about."

"Keep your signal down or you'll have every cleanser and building unit coming over."

But it was too late. A semicircle of curious machines had already formed by the lake.

"Go away you pests. Shoo!" ordered the statue by the lake haughtily. "This is a private conversation."

Reluctantly, with squeaking wheels and dustpans dragging on the ground, the lower castes trundled off. The two statues then changed to less noticeable shades of maroon and olive and settled down to listen to the saga of the matrix boxes.

24

Calmly, methodically, the Drune made its way about the gloom of its secret laboratory. With icy detachment it set in motion the countdown that would culminate in the launch of its patchwork missile. Then it left to disengage the fuel lines and check it over one last time. It was going to work and no one, above or below, was going to prevent it.

The Drune returned to its control, at last able to clean its aching body and change its clothes. Then, with meticulous efficiency, it locked the multi-headed missile into a firing sequence, which would launch it automatically through the crust of the planet, and towards its target. The Drune noticed that the movement of the crust had shifted the launch tunnel a few centimetres, but not enough to interfere with the rocket's trajectory. The Drune reached out and threw the last switch.

Somewhere in the middle of a vast dry wilderness two onagers stopped grazing to watch a large circle of sand disappear. The rest of the herd foraging a short way off wandered cautiously over to take a look. It wasn't a well shaft, oil or otherwise. There were no humans within miles so it couldn't be another war, and even educated camels lacked the ability to dig holes. The asses scraped the ground and occasionally bit their neighbour in annoyance and confusion. Should they allow curiosity to become the better part of common sense? It could have been a trap to catch wild onagers.

Fortunately for them their indecision was resolved by a horrible screaming wail from the bowels of the Earth. Every living creature within miles evacuated its wallow, burrow and scrape. By the time an ascending rumble issued from the hole there was nothing around to hear it.

The search by Walton and the Atlantians was suddenly halted as a wailing scream vibrated through the solid and fluid rock. It sounded like the caterwauling of ten thousand sabre-toothed tigers in heat. The more recognizable roar of the launched rocket and its upward rumble momentarily froze their capacity to think.

Having seen nuclear weapons tested, Walton counted out the potential yield of the stolen missiles only to visualize the charred radioactive remains of a planet. The ulcer he hadn't felt for five years started to do a jig. It no longer mattered if Rabette had been baked in a pie with four-and-twenty blackbirds.

Not so bound to the great above, the Atlantians started to chatter excitedly in their own tongue. Walton tightened his abdomen muscles in the hope the lining of his stomach would drop back into place and he started to operate his grey matter in a way that gave his pomposity a fright. All missiles were controlled from a base of some sort and even the Drune must have given it a self-destruct facility. Most probably, it had used the rocket's space capacity to take it into an orbit where no land based anti missile system could reach it. The lasers and killer satellites already in space were still being tested and the only successes they had clocked up for years were diverting several communication satellites, and shattering each others' mirrors.

If the warhead was going into orbit before dispatching its missiles they might have time to continue the search for the Drune's control now they had some vibrations to follow.

The reaction of the rest of the human species was less agitated. Principally because, like most things that are liable to dramatically affect everyone on the planet, the news was suppressed by those who knew best. The only thing the major powers could be sanguine about was that the Other Side had not launched the warhead, even though parts of the device had once belonged to both of them. With baited breath and targeted interceptors surveillance crews waited for it to come into range, and they waited, and waited . . .

The Drune crouched in the spangled darkness of its control, immobile and strangely secure. Slowly it switched off each panel, monitor and circuit as though saying goodbye to a dear friend. They had been its faithful sentinels and silent army.

Finally it came to the globe. The Drune found it impossible to pass it by without one last hallucination to relieve the turmoil in its mind. Urging its brain to release only its kindest memories, the renegade lifted its hands, but the kindest memory was of that small pale creature in the tartan suit. With frightening familiarity, a living, animated Rabette smiled back at the Drune from the throbbing depths of its mind. Why didn't he scowl? Why didn't he curse like an ordinary mortal?

The Drune couldn't bear to watch and the apparition left.

A girl and boy came into focus through the globe's bubbles of light. They were strolling in a quiet park. Apart from the buzz of pollinating insects in the bowers of blossom and tall stems of lilies, their secret conversation was all that broke the silence.

They came to a softly rippling brook. Lying on a cushion of moss beneath the shade of low branches was an elegant figure clad in richly embroidered green and gold. Apparently fast asleep in its secluded paradise, one of its hands skimmed the water and the other lay across its chest. The young couple stopped in delight.

"Oh how beautiful," whispered the boy.

The girl knelt beside the sleeper. "Few could have been this close to it. I've never seen anything so exquisite."

"We should keep away though."

"There's no one else about and it's fast asleep."

"But still . . ."

"You won't tell on me if I touch it, will you?"

"Well, of course not. But really, you shouldn't."

"What rubbish. Hold our flowers will you." She passed him their bouquet of water roses so enthusiastically he was pricked by their thorns. Swiftly and gently she pressed her lips to those of the sleeper.

"Oh, Ola!" gasped the boy.

"It's gorgeous, it smells so fragrant. You try it as well."

"Oh, all right." He took his friend's place and repeated the compliment. "Now I suppose we must both be criminals."

They laughed. The boy pulled a thornless bloom from the flowers and tucked it in the hand of the slumbering figure. Then they both darted guiltily on their way.

As the supposed sleeper heard them go, it smiled contentedly and held the flower to its lips.

The unruffled image of paradise slowly faded. In place of it appeared that benignly smiling ginger cat.

"What is wrong, Silver Ver Drene?"

The Drune backed away from the globe. "Don't call me that."

"What? You've denied your mortality, you've denied your friends, and now you deny your name?"

"I will admit to murder and treachery and am working on madness."

Jane Palmer

"Madness?"

"I suffer from too much sanity. I'm afraid of madness, but I don't want to stay sane."

"Why must you be mad?"

"Am I not talking to myself?"

"Who else could you hold an intelligent conversation with?"

"Leave me alone."

"We have more power than you believe."

"We?"

"You, me and those thoughts you try to deny."

"What thoughts?"

"The ones you will not share with me."

In a spasm of terror the Drune snatched up the black cover and threw it over the globe. What was happening to its subconscious? If these weren't the symptoms of madness then its thoughts were being invaded by a smug ginger cat.

The Drune dashed from the chamber and into a waiting capsule, only hesitating to bring down the heavy shutter sealing the complex.

25

After tracking the source of the vibrations that had made the planet ring like a bell for some while, the leading capsule suddenly stopped. Walton and the Atlantians waited in the shadow of the tunnel junction to watch the Drune's craft float swiftly by.

"We'd do better to follow the Drune," Walton whispered into his communicator.

So they carefully pursued Pyg's minion at a safe distance, through chambers, tunnels, watercourses and the occasional city. At last they entered Rosipolees from under a lake. By the balcony where the lift went down to Pyg's control, the Drune's craft hung suspended like a wingless bird, hovering between attack and flight. Worried that it could notice them before leading the way to its mistress, the Atlantians dropped their capsules to the floor of the city, where they merged into the shadows.

They waited. Eventually there was a movement, but not from above. A large black woman ambled casually towards them, apparently from nowhere.

"I thought this place was deserted?" Walton asked.

"It has been for thousands of years," Anniya told him. "Of course, that must be Akaylia. But how did she get down here?"

"Think I should ask her?"

"As long as you stay low the Drune shouldn't see you."

Having learnt the value of stealth the hard way, Walton used the cover of walkways and walls to join the interloper by a statue.

"Who the hell are you?" he demanded.

"Akaylia Jackson." She beamed and extended her hand.

"I didn't mean that. I meant, what are you doing down here?"

"Why shouldn't I be down here? I'm a geologist. What are you, prissy pants?"

"Walton Clarke, an astronomer."

"Well you're the one who took the wrong turning, you colossal cuckoo."

"This is hardly the time and place to argue."

"My sentiment exactly."

"But what *are* you doing down here?"

Akaylia looked the tall, distinguished intruder up and down thoughtfully. "I was going to warn you against something but I can see that you're the sort that wants proof in plural before taking somebody's word for anything."

"Warn me against what?"

"Against following that silver spider into its mistress's web."

"But we must."

"I was right."

"We have to find the control for the missile and abort it before it can deploy its warheads."

"There isn't any need."

Walton was silent for a moment. He was open minded enough to turn over several possibilities for her optimism, but none of them would fit the jigsaw his own experiences had constructed. "Of course there is."

"You've been duped, big fellow."

He considered that very unlikely. His students were trying it on all the while. But this wasn't a small matter of magenta mould or perpetual motion. "How? Duped?"

"What's going on isn't really what you think."

Coming from a character like Akaylia Jackson, that didn't have the smallest ring of plausibility. However, he decided not to argue. "And Rabette is missing. Doesn't that bother you?"

Akaylia rolled her head and thought carefully. "You won't take my word for it then?"

"I'm afraid I can't – whatever you're doing down here."

"What about her opinion?" She indicated the pink pulsating statue that had been listening to the conversation with keen interest.

"What's a fancy glass vase got to do with it?"

The statue was quite indignant. "I am not a vase. This shape indicates my conversational level."

"Good God!" Walton exclaimed, too loudly for comfort. "What the hell are you?"

"God or hell has nothing to do with my actuation. I am supplied by the city memory bank. What is it you wish to discuss?"

Although taken aback, Walton managed to ask, "What is she talking about?"

"Self preservation. She is simply saying that it would not be safe to follow the Drune."

"None of us expected it would be."

"Perhaps the risk outweighs the benefit."

The Drune's craft still hung motionless by the entrance above. Walton realised he had time to defeat Akaylia's argument by another ploy.

"So you know everything do you?"

"Everything that is required to make rational conversation," the pink statue replied.

"So why don't you tell me a few things about this place?"

"Of course."

"How old is the Atlantian civilization?"

"Atlantians? They are pure mythology."

"I see," muttered Walton.

Akaylia started to drum her fingers against the statue in an attempt to make it keep quiet, but it liked answering questions and found the vibrations unusually pleasing.

"Who are those people over there in those capsules then?"

The statue's long thin proboscis swung regally into the air to take an objective look.

"Ossiane engineers of course. They should be refurbishing our cities for the tourists, but I don't know what came over them. They suddenly started dashing around in capsules and putting out volcanoes. Totally silly I call it. The pressure in some of those magma chambers gives them terrible headaches and the volcanoes erupt somewhere else anyway. One or two of us on the higher levels have ended up paddling in lava. We're not designed for it you know. I mean – underfloor heating is all very well above ground, but down here we prefer it a little cooler. But that was something they did get round to before they thought they were rocket propelled moles. Whole new unit full of freon they built. Got a crystal dome, twenty spires and stands on legs like a potentate's tomb. Would you like a guided tour?"

Walton was suddenly aware that the pink vase had stopped chattering and expected a reply. "You mean there are some of you who can actually walk about? No thank you!" To prevent it gabbling on about volcanoes and central heating he asked without warning, "Tell me how to stop the Drune's missile?"

The long proboscis scratched its neckless head thoughtfully. It was beginning to realize that the visitor only liked direct answers and had probably been starved of rational conversation for a dangerous length of time. "Oh well, if you insist." Akaylia fetched its plinth a swift kick and with a pulse of bright purple it shut up.

"I should have known," sighed Walton. "Rabette was right. Crazy Akaylia! And she's found a friend to join her." He strolled away.

"What did I tell you about answering any questions other than the ones I told you to, you pink potted pinhead?" Akaylia snarled at the statue when he was out of earshot.

"But I was trying to be honest."

"Some mortals can only take the truth in small doses. You've given him enough resistance to it to last him years. You'd make a better parking meter."

"What's that?"

"You'll find out when the tourists come, talkative treasure."

The Drune was leaving its capsule and stepping into a lift cage. Stealthily Walton and the Atlantians followed it down to Pyg's control. Akaylia gave a deep sigh. It looked as though the thinking and heroic stuff was going to be down to her after all.

"Of course," the conversation piece went on. "Perhaps if I had introduced a little culture into the conversation he might have been more interested."

"You can't sidetrack astronomers who are used to the idea of supernova wiping away galactic arms with snippets about culture."

"What about the music of the spheres?"

"You are beginning to become a pain."

"Whereabouts?"

"Right in the stem, where I'll knee you any moment now."

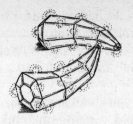

26

Slowly, resolutely, the Drune strode into Pyg's chamber. Its purple eyes were wide and defiant.

Pyg was amused and surprised. "Come back? You've come back Drune?"

"Who else in this planet have you left with enough wit to push a lift button?"

"And in your best tunic. Which one of us has something to celebrate?"

As the Drune was aware, Pyg had the fortunate state of mind to regret nothing. It knew it was the one who should be flinching, but it was beyond such subtle feelings, and Pyg sensed it.

For brevity's sake she could have stunned it then and there to concentrate on her ship's countdown. The fact that it was so immaculately dressed in gold and green for the occasion made her hesitate.

"What do you want?" she asked.

"Not to hear your malicious scratching tones. I came to tell you that I used the Ossianes' primary survey tunnel to launch the missile which will deflect the comet."

"I know."

Pyg had obviously been aware of what it was up to all

along. Every follicle on the Drune's body froze in horror. It dare not find out more, so it never spoke.

"You had quite a problem meeting the deadline for its right trajectory didn't you."

Any inclination to continue playing the android seeped away. The Drune clenched its fists and even Pyg couldn't miss the spark of loathing glistening in its eyes.

"I betrayed you. I would have killed you if I'd known how."

"I knew you were trying to deceive me from the beginning, Silver Ver Drene, but you were interesting to study. Why did you have to think me such a fool?"

"I had to. I was the only one down here to escape your 'alternative reality'."

Pyg laughed so heartily she was unable to speak.

"You!" she eventually whirred. "The very creature treated by its own kind as an abomination. For those bigoted, self-satisfied hypocrites and a race of humans you never knew you were prepared to sacrifice the only thing you loved. I honestly didn't think you had the strength to go through with it." The Drune closed its eyes in pain. "Yes, I knew how much you thought of that little creature. You, a genderless untouchable. Ossianes only allowed 'love' between sexual partners, and you are a neuter, Chief Technical Adviser. Why did you have to limit your vast potential by something as petty as emotion?"

"After becoming your knave, what was left? I connived with an alien to manipulate this planet."

"Don't assume the arrogance of suffering my guilt for me. You know quite well you had no choice in the matter."

"I needn't have killed Rabette."

"How could you know I would have allowed you to launch that rocket?"

"I should have realised you were bluffing."

"Why? I've never bluffed about anything before."

"Let me have Rabette's body."

"Not now. It's down in the matrix frozen solid. I'll program the machines to shrink the harmless gnat and mount it in amber so you can wear it on a chain."

At last the Drune's recalcitrant tongue was silenced. It covered its face and turned away.

Pyg should have felt smug but her satisfaction was strangely thin. "I found this all quite fascinating. Our species seldom bother making emotional bonds. The young are born so small they have to be incubated in a machine. Perhaps if your mother hadn't been so fond of her child – unlike Rabette's who surrendered it to the authorities the minute it was born – your logic would have overruled any irrational obligation. But why so proud? What divine mechanic gave you the strength to look alien monsters like me in the eye and never flinch? What enigma fuels that mental fortress? Whatever it is, it'd be worth setting up another experiment on this scale to find out."

Pyg rested back, her callousness now sufficiently restored to allow her to bask in the success of her research.

"Your remarkable performance supplied the best data of the whole planet, Silver Ver Drene. You were superb. The Ossianes had contempt for you when they knew you were one of them, and terror when they believed you weren't. The shame is, they will never know the truth. If they were returned tomorrow they would carry on treating you in the same way. We should give you something to compensate for Rabette, though. After all, there was no need to destroy the little creature was there. Let's see . . . What can we offer you? How about half of Ossiane? I'll leave the main monitor connected so you can play with it to your heart's content. Or all of Ossiane if you like. It doesn't matter to us anyway now the planet's not going to be demolished by that comet after all. I've no doubt you could do something interesting with it."

The Drune swayed slightly.

"You can have control of this complex as well; atmosphere generators, power convertors, shielding – everything!" Then she pondered. "I'd ask you to come with us but you wouldn't survive the cryogenic chamber either, and nobody would ever know you made the sacrifice for the sake of your charade. Well? What do you want?"

The Drune was silent for some while.

It eventually asked, "Destroy me."

Pyg was taken aback. "Destroy you? Why should I destroy you?"

"You promised to make me plead to be destroyed."

"I know, but that didn't mean I was going to do it."

"I betrayed you."

"I know. Your expertise in going about it was quite fascinating. Besides, there are bound to be teeth marks when dealing with experimental animals."

"I hate you."

"That's understandable enough. A normal reaction."

"I'm losing my reason."

"Possibly you are, Silver Ver Drene. I'm not going to kill you though. You worked too hard to keep those humans and your ungrateful species alive – and I've grown rather fond of you."

"Where is the kindness in sparing one of your experimental animals when the vivisection is over?"

"All right." Pyg found the strength to admit, "I respect you too much."

"Please don't! Hate me instead."

"Hate you? I'm a scientist, not a human being." Pyg pressed a switch on her chair and a compartment in the dais opened. In it were three bland boxes containing two large, glittering jewels. "Look, I'll even let you bring the Ossianes back to their senses; back to their pompous prejudices." The Drune looked up sharply in disbelief. "When we've gone of course." Then Pyg became exasperated. "Did you honestly believe you could challenge someone millions of years more advanced and come out of it unscathed?" She gave up. "We're wasting precious time. You know my species does not suffer from guilt or pity. What is it you want of me?"

"The Ealinan reward for faithless service."

"I never intended to destroy you. Your mind is too valuable to switch off. You must learn to live with yourself."

27

Walton turned awkwardly to study the baffled expressions of the others. What were Pyg and the Drune talking about? It was obviously important. Walton indicated that it was time to confront them. As they shared so few traits of character with the astronomer, especially grim determination, the Atlantians started to wonder whether his mental condition had something to do with his size. The only use they could find for it was as a shield when they gingerly made their ways after him.

Pyg wasn't surprised when the motley bunch strode past the open shutter. The Drune never moved. It was not only suffering from guilt, but severe anti-climax and wanted to sink though the moho with a whimper.

"Oh look," Pyg told it. "Some friends have come to find you."

Walton seized the Drune's arm and spun it round to face him. "Where is Rabette?"

"I killed him."

Walton's hands were on its throat in the same second but, before they could close round its neck, Pyg explained, "That's what Silver Ver Drene wanted. You'll only make yourself a murderer for the sake of doing it a favour. I tried to explain what a waste it would be."

Hesitantly Walton released his grip. Not an executioner at heart, he pushed the Drune aside.

"How much do you remember, Doctor Clarke?" asked Pyg.

"Not much."

"Well excuse me not going into detail. There isn't time. The Drune might have told you if you had been nicer to it."

"I know those warheads are about to strike pretty soon."

"Goodness no," laughed Pyg. "That will take five months at least."

Whatever else Walton had been mistaken about, he was noted for the accuracy of his mathematical estimations. He counted them out again on his mental fingers; time of launch, highest possible orbit and firing sequence. They must already have been on their way but, in that case, why was Pyg carrying on such a simplistic conversation with intellects she must have found tedious.

Walton put his mental abacus away. "What do you mean?"

"It will take that long for the rocket to reach the comet on collision course with this planet."

For a moment Walton was more indignant at the thought of someone discovering it before him than alarmed at what it could do.

"What comet?"

"The one you astronomers and your fancy telescopes won't be able to see for another month, by which time they would not be able to do anything about it. If it hadn't been for Silver Ver Drene, your planet would soon have had a sizable hole punched in it."

"What?"

"You may or may not believe it, Doctor, but that creature you ungraciously offered to throttle has just saved your world with the rocket you so desperately tried to stop it launching."

"That?" Walton stabbed a finger at the Drune.

"I would advise you to treat it with care, but your sudden arrival has left me with no alternative. I'm sorry." Pyg pushed a button on the monitor control, then rose.

Pyg's full height was half as much again as Walton's. His grim determination retreated at the sight of it and the Atlantians irregularly closed ranks behind him. A large empty chamber in one of the walls was suddenly illuminated.

"After all I promised Silver Ver Drene, it seems heartless to do this to it, but we Ealinans were never that sentimental." Knowing what was about to happen, the Drune tried to bolt for the entrance but Pyg raised the flashing button on her palm and stunned it. "Pick it up, Doctor, and carry it into the chamber. All you others join them. I'm afraid it would be too risky having any of you wandering about during our countdown. You might crop up in the wrong place and frighten the Captain."

Walton realised that Pyg was controlling his movements. "What are you going to do?"

"Nothing too unpleasant or painful. You might find it a little boring, but I'm sure all of you could do with the rest." She adjusted a control on the monitor. "I'll set it for a couple of months. That won't do you any harm, although I'm afraid Silver Ver Drene might be beyond explaining anything by then. It's bound to be quite mad by the time you're released. You will give it a good home though, won't you?"

Slowly the Atlantians, Walton and the Drune were

drawn back into the chamber by some implacable force. Then a clear screen was lowered before them. As though frozen in ice, all they could do was listen to their spinning thoughts.

Pyg listened as well. Despite her former haste to leave she sat down and concentrated. Then she smiled. The reason why Ealinans never formed emotional bonds was probably because their mouths had evolved under their chins and they could never tell what each other were thinking. But Pyg's smile was a private affair anyway.

Pyg leisurely tapped her control and ordered the Captain to put the ship into its final countdown. She watched the monitors on her panel with amused curiosity. Her amusement didn't last long. One monitor was now registering something, which transformed her smile into a double chin.

If Pyg's eyes were not already fearsome enough, they would have acquired a noticeable malevolence as her control panel at last winked out the warning she should have received hours before. Whatever had burrowed its way through to the matrix had done its selective damage and left. Not accustomed to feeling intimidated herself, the sensation of trepidation tingling its way up her long spine was a novel experience. She didn't bother to ponder whether this was the reaction she managed to give others, and punched open the channel to the matrix sentinel. It didn't answer. That must have been the first thing the mechanical mouse had nibbled through. Not wanting to go below and risk descending into a trap, Pyg decided to order down some of the crew, but before she could do so a dark figure stood beyond the chamber shutter. Pyg looked harder, then opened the palm of her hand to stun it. Whether ghost or mortal, if it was indigenous it was hardly likely to be friendly.

The intruder ambled forward. There could be no doubting that Pyg was confronting a very annoyed human about to demand what she had been doing to her planet.

Pyg raised her palm.

"I wouldn't do that if I were you." Akaylia suddenly acquired a pulsating halo. "The energy would only be reflected. Could give your pearly complexion a hint of crisp."

Pyg lowered her palm. "Well," she eventually clicked. "How did you manage it? How did you override the sentinel?"

"You never bothered to chat to a conversation piece, did you?"

"I've had other things on my mind."

"Well, if you had, you would have realized that the city's computer has an illogic circuit." Akaylia smiled. "My speciality. Easily convinced it that the alien maggot, which had burrowed into the world's crust, would metamorphose into a gravitational anomaly that could fall through to the other side of the planet."

Pyg gave a cynical whirr. "You convinced a computer with an argument like that?"

"It's only the equipment it controls that answers back."

"I had the same trouble with this grey model."

Akaylia saw the captives behind the screen. "Draining a few batteries, I see."

"The species of this planet are a very clumsy piece of apparatus."

"I've no doubt yours used to have ears and noses at some time."

"Many other appendages as well."

"Did away with everything bar the poison sac."

"Oh dear, you aren't going to accuse me of being a reptile as well?"

"Goodness no. Down here they evicted them from the sewers centuries ago."

"I wonder if I should take your word that you control so much of this complex?"

"Come outside and I'll show you." Pyg was immediately suspicious so Akaylia went on. "Not enough to crumple your ship or give you a conscience, but I could make your take off very messy."

"I don't believe you."

"I could open a few shutters. Alter the pressure inside the hill."

"Prove it."

"Come outside."

Reluctantly Pyg rose. With half a step she came down from her dais and with six more was at the entrance. Akaylia led her into the lift and up to the balcony where it was possible to look down on the dimly lit Rosipolees.

"Well, what would you like? A parade of conversation pieces?" Akaylia knew Pyg's tongue would make short work of them. "Change in the atmospheric pressure?"

"No." Pyg's thin bones could snap long before Akaylia's well-upholstered frame even started to register the change.

"Firework display?" Pyg loured suspiciously at the suggestion and Akaylia happily raised her hands to announce. "Lighting on maximum."

Something bleeped in annoyance.

"Shut up parsnip pot."

The mechanic rattled its case in irritation.

Pyg had the self-control not to turn and see what the bad-tempered entity looked like. Instead, she watched the city below clothe itself in a shimmering gown of light. As its designers had once intended, the vista vibrated colour like a three-dimensional stained glass window. Light throbbed from below every floor, pavement and bridge. The occasional shattering of wafer thin obsidian was heard because windows, millennia old, could not withstand the sudden heat of the illumination.

"You could start a fire," warned Pyg.

"Oh that's all right," Akaylia smiled. "I can reduce the oxygen."

"No," snapped Pyg.

Akaylia raised her hands again. "Bring it down to half light." She turned to Pyg. "As much as this planet has found your company a novelty, perhaps it would be in order to ask when you intend to leave?"

"The ship is in countdown."

"Good."

Pyg hesitated. "You intend to let the ship leave?"

Akaylia shrugged. "Why not? What would we do with you? You'll never return. You've had your fun and I don't want anyone from your planet to come looking for you, and there's even a chance you met your match."

Pyg laughed. "You mean the Drune?"

"It could have taken you out at any time."

"Perhaps; it had the best excavating machines and work robots this planet has ever seen, not to mention the genius. Unfortunately it also suffered from compassion and I held all the Ossianes hostage." It was obvious the city's atmospheric pressure was making Pyg uncomfortable.

"Shall we go back to your lair?"

Although it meant turning her back on Akaylia and the bleeping machine, Pyg returned. At a safe distance, Akaylia followed the alien to her control chamber. "All right, I think it's time you went."

Pyg hesitated. "You will be careful when you isolate the matrix below, won't you. There is more power running through there than the instruments register."

"It's booby trapped?"

"What makes you think that? Perhaps we should trust each other?"

"I'll trust you when you're on the other side of this galaxy."

"Aren't we two of a kind?"

"Are we?"

"I'm sure of it. At least I never pretended to be a buffoon. You did have me fooled, you know."

"Perhaps if you had a few of those superfluous appendages grafted back on, your perceptions might increase."

"I doubt it. Protruding things like noses, ear lobes and consciences can be so very inconvenient."

"There is nothing which would make you think twice about anything is there?"

"I must confess I have this partiality for poetic justice, but then, we all have our little weaknesses."

"Poetic justice?"

Pyg tapped a key on her control panel and a door in the seamless wall slid aside. "Now, you will have to excuse me. I've no doubt your pet mechanic has managed to shut down the primary units. Do wait until we've gone, though, before waking anyone up. You wouldn't want to see them mangled during our take off would you." She stepped into the lift. "Goodbye Akaylia Jackson."

"Sleep tight," snarled Akaylia. "Then it won't hurt so much if you collide with an asteroid."

The door silently slid back and muffled Pyg's reply.

The mechanic bleeped. "What had all that got to do with engineering?"

Akaylia frowned. "Don't get cute unless you want a few nuts and bolts loosened."

"Nuts and bolts? You'll find all my parts are laser welded."

Akaylia wondered why she was trying to argue with a bad-tempered machine when she could have been thinking up some way to scupper the alien ship before it left the planet's atmosphere. A small voice told her it would be a lost cause. Neither the technology nor engineering existed any more. Pyg's visit had come expensive. She looked at the collection of captives, motionless like fish in a frozen fountain, and suspected one or two of them were not going to like it when they woke up.

28

Once again, Uncle Arthur held up the needle to the light of the window and tried to thread it with his rheumatic fingers. That infernal bumping, grinding and throbbing from the hillside was playing havoc with his biological gyroscope. He had no doubt it was caused by the aliens under the lake, but they were not the sort of folk you knocked on the door to complain to. Perhaps they had kidnapped another scientist and were celebrating the occasion.

The frantic newscasts were howling out what governments had been trying to conceal – that a massive multiple warhead had been launched from the bowels of the Earth – and it only made him prick his finger. But when someone started to roll away the underside of the nearest hill, Arthur's concentration was completely shattered. He may have lost the battle with the military over his old farm but he'd be damned if he allowed some alien to drive him off this one.

He threw the needle, thread and sock into the workbasket and unlocked his shotgun. After loading both barrels he pulled on his boots and stomped out with the intention of discovering if aliens were bullet proof.

Compelling his stiff limbs to the top of the hill, Arthur glowered down at the waters of the muddy lake. Beneath him the rumbling and grating noises carried on unremittingly as though a huge barrier were being drawn aside. Then something massive slid from the hill and into the murky depths.

Uncle Arthur tucked the shotgun under his arm so he could fumble for his glasses. Then he watched as the vast expanse of water went down, as though someone had just pulled out a plug in the bowels of the hill. Soon, a wide shore was revealed, littered with years of rubbish that had been hurled into the lake from the bank, and the remaining water started to bubble.

The farmer cocked his shotgun. No longer murky, the centre of the lake was slowly filled by acres of pulsating lights. Arthur nearly toppled from his vantage point.

Realizing the shotgun was useless in a situation like this, he let the weapon fall. As it slid down the slope, a twig caught the trigger and fired both barrels over his head. He didn't flinch, just kept staring at the show below.

Eventually the water stopped bubbling and the lights began to flash in sequence as the remains of the lake surrendered its monster. A few rivulets of water slid away from its satin skin as a vast circular craft presented itself to the sky. The top was a smooth and gently curved but, as it rose, a montage of irregular prominences were clinging to it underside like so many baby marsupials on the belly of their mother. Arthur half expected one to detach itself at any second to come and say goodbye, but the parent was calling the tune, albeit a noiseless one. For all the racket it had made, swivelling itself out of the hill and into the lake, it now ascended into the sky more silently than a hunting kestrel.

Gradually all the appendages on the monster's stomach started to rotate. The resulting spectacle disorientated

Arthur, so much so that he lost his balance and sat down where he was. Something told him that if the contraption was about to take off he should get up and run, but he felt as though he were glued to the spot. Even the hard corners of a tobacco tin he was sitting on were no incentive to make him move.

A cylinder of brilliant light suddenly flashed down from the centre of the craft. Though it didn't so much as ripple the remaining water of the lake there was enough power in it to punch the mighty visitor heavenward. Dizzy, and amazingly unsinged, Uncle Arthur watched it vanish straight up to become a speck in the sky. Then, with a short burst of brilliance, it was gone.

It was a good while before the farmer decided to move. Eventually he eased himself upright to totter down the slope and retrieve the gun that had almost shot him. Carefully wiping away the grime he made his way back to the summit where he stood watching for another half an hour. The lake was still almost empty, though where the water had gone he could only guess. Several cracks had appeared in the rock and, realizing what that meant, Arthur scrambled back down to his farm as quickly as he could. Something told his hardened senses that the show was not quite over.

He made himself a thermos of coffee and whisky, took it to the roofless Landrover, rolled himself a cigarette, then sat down on the straw in the back of the vehicle to watch. In the meantime those embryo cracks had been maturing. It seemed that whatever had been supporting the hill had left with the spacecraft. There was nothing regular or mechanical about the rumbling this time. It was Nature taking her course with cruel predictability. Arthur had the feeling he should grab any valuables and make off before it was too late, but even his intractable disposition had its inquisitive side.

The rim where he had stood started to disappear first.

Slowly it crumbled inwards. As each section of the hill's summit vanished it was accompanied by a resounding splash inside its hollow interior.

"So that's where all the water went to," Arthur mused to himself.

The show went on for several hours until there was nothing left of the hill at all. Looking through the gap where it had been, Arthur could see the lake was back to its normal level.

"Nice view," he decided with the first approval he had shown for anything in years. "Only hope it don't attract tourists."

Reasonably satisfied with the outcome, he swallowed the dregs of the thermos, kicked some smouldering straw, which had been set on fire by his cigarettes, out of the Landrover, and went back to the bungalow.

Once more he attempted to thread his needle.

29

Akaylia intently watched the monitors on Pyg's control panel. She hoped Walton and the Ossianes would not dash out of their prison when they came to their senses, as she intended to discharge the energy of the matrix into the alien's chamber in case she had left some booby trap. Even a small puncture in the shielding of the city above could have depressurized it. That would have immediately made Rosipolees crumple into a narrow band of interesting elements in the burning basalt. And the geologist wasn't inclined to rely on the reports of the mechanical surveyors Rosipolees' computer occasionally sent out. If they had been talking to any conversation pieces they were bound to be unreliable.

The mechanic was not happy with Akaylia's solution. "Releasing that sort of power in here could damage the equipment."

"Releasing it into the city could flatten the region, parsnip pot. There are plenty of engineers about to stabilize everything." The mechanic bleeped in offence. "And you of course. Set up a safety screen for them as well, just in case."

"Perhaps I'm not programmed to tinker with alien engineering."

"After the way we've rearranged this place between us, it's a fine time to decide that, bombastic box."

When the Drune saw the flashing white fronds of energy fill the chamber it plunged into them. With arms raised it drew the discharged power but an invisible shell protected the Drune and it was delineated in a shimmering halo.

The others watched in frozen amazement from the safety of their cell. At first the Ossianes were convinced that the Drune was quite mad, then they felt Pyg's illusion dribble away. They were the ones who had been deranged and rearranged. They looked up at Akaylia, standing on the dais. The Drune, seeing that the mechanic beside her had created the protective field, lowered its arms in disappointment as the energy filtered away.

How could the others have failed to recognize Ossiane's Chief Technical Adviser?

"Now I remember what happened to Silver Ver Drene," Anniya suddenly blurted out. "It was banished because it frightened a few senile autocrats."

"Of course," another engineer recalled. "It was imprisoned in Rosipolees."

"Can you help the mechanic shut down the rest of the alien's equipment, Silver Ver Drene?" asked Akaylia.

By the expression in the Drune's eyes it was impossible to tell whether the request had registered. It darted a half-startled, half-artful glance to either side of it then slowly walked towards the dais. Suddenly the mechanic began to bleep a warning.

"What's the matter with you now?" demanded Akaylia.

"Keep that creature away from me!" it screeched in near mortal alarm.

"Why?"

"Believe me. My perceptions are more finely tuned than yours."

"But Anniya says it's the Ossianes' Chief Technical Adviser," protested Walton.

"It is also mad."

The Drune suddenly stopped. It sensed that the mechanic was arming itself. At the same time, Akaylia was becoming exasperated. "It's not usual for mortals to attack robots."

"I can defend myself, but don't let it near that control panel."

With a cat-like bound the Drune leapt onto the dais and stood menacingly beside the equipment.

Now Akaylia was worried.

"I think that alien must have unbalanced its mind," Walton told her.

Akaylia suddenly realised. "Oh no, it's not the alien it wants revenge on, but the planet."

"But Silver Ver Drene risked its life to save it."

"When it was sane."

The Drune's purple eyes opened wider and it inclined its head slightly to one side.

Walton cautiously came forward. "You weren't to blame about Rabette," he insisted as reasonably as he could, considering he was not sure himself.

The Drune smiled icily and reached out a hand to Pyg's control panel. Possibly the action was just to alarm the others, but Akaylia was taking no chances.

"Stun it," she ordered the mechanic.

Before the Drune could touch anything a small globe of lemon light was propelled at its head. It toppled from the dais and Walton caught it.

"I'm sure it didn't mean any harm," the astronomer apologized thinly.

"At this depth I'm prepared to immobilize anyone who so much as gets the hiccups."

"I think Pyg made it kill Rabette."

One of the senior engineers stepped forward. "It's never

been totally sane. It's always had a spark of madness in its eyes. We should never have had to depend so much on a no-gender of course, but normal Ossiane genes don't seem to carry that amount of genius."

Walton was still having difficulty taking everything in.

"Just who are you?" he demanded.

"Engineers," Anniya said quickly.

Then the truth dawned on Walton. "You've been con-ning me, haven't you? You, the only surviving Atlantians? Come off it. Where are the rest of your people?"

"I don't know, Walton, I swear. The alien must have been controlling our minds. The Drune is the only one who can tell you that."

"But it's mad. And just what is it? It's not like you?"

"It's a no-gender. They are strange creatures – our third sex. They are only allowed to wear green and gold. Silver Ver Drene obviously developed a taste for black. Would probably have turned into a spider given long enough."

The Drune's eyes flickered open. It pushed itself from Walton's grasp. Lemon must have had a rationalizing effect on its mind. It looked a good deal saner, but the strain of maintaining its performance as an android had been too much. Silver Ver Drene was once again aware of the intolerance that had almost driven it mad. It loosened the high collar of the green tunic and could feel the cold chill as its soul once more went under the heel of its own species' contempt.

"What is bothering you?" Akaylia asked.

"I want the illusion Pyg gave everyone else. A quiet hell to live in. Rhyme me an illusion."

"While you played your game of mouse and cat
I went and altered the thermostat."

Akaylia pushed a button on Pyg's control panel, causing

183

the cryogenic chamber to rotate slowly up through the floor. As the door slid open, there sat Rabette, soggy, shivering and glowering daggers at the Drune.

> "I altered everything I could get at,
> Including the cryogenic thermostat."

The Drune swayed slightly, looked disbelievingly at Akaylia, then at Rabette. The small creature's expression was not a forgiving one.

"Well say something, Silver Hair," demanded Akaylia.

"You're an awful poet."

"I'm cold," protested Rabette.

Akaylia released him from the cryogenic chamber.

"I suppose you thought that was funny," Rabette snapped at the Drune. "I could have had a cardiac arrest."

Then Silver Ver Drene realised that Pyg hadn't been lying about Rabette. By the way its small companion had shaved back his ruff of neck hair the Drune should have guessed that he too was a no-gender.

"You might have at least told me you altered the thermostat. I nearly died with fright. Say something damn you!"

But the Drune was preoccupied.

"No devil from our past must ever trick us again, Silver Hair," Akaylia told it.

"We will always be tricked. We live, die and circle dimensions like tops. We change illusions too willingly, like coats."

"A dissident Drune."

"Don't mock me."

"Why should I, Silver Hair?"

"Everyone who is able to live at noon mocks those born at midnight. Contempt needs no excuses. And I maintained the machines that transmitted the Atlantian illusion and collected Pyg's data on humans."

"Traitor," murmured an Ossiane engineer.

"Pyg had the capacity to exterminate everything on this planet if I hadn't co-operated. Now nothing matters any more. Once I wanted to build palaces in the clouds, but I was only allowed to design hallowed Ossiane complexes I would never be allowed to enter. I lied to myself so I could stay sane. I wore the green and gold and pretended that those I was forbidden to touch really respected me. But we were all liars."

"No," protested Walton. "Think of what Pyg's species must be like."

The Drune laughed. "Oh, I knew her species well. Their idea of altruism was evolved from Tyrannosaurus Rex. They are cruel, logical and so technically advanced they don't have to bother with compassion, but they are not hypocrites."

"What are you talking about?"

"Pyg respected me. She knew I was betraying her, yet had more regard for me than the whole of Ossiane."

Then the Drune's anger seeped away into confusion. It suddenly seemed to grow smaller like a glistening snail withdrawing into its silver shell.

"What happened?" asked Akaylia.

"Pyg found Rosipolees. She was able to read the Ossiane language, but didn't realize the plaque warning against releasing me from stasis referred to a living being: Drunes have always been referred to as objects, mere things. At first she thought I must be a biological android which had to be kept oxygenated. I had to be some use to her or she would have destroyed me. Pyg somehow realised that I cared about Rabette." The Drune turned to the Ossianes. "You won't harm him, will you?"

"Why should we?" asked Anniya.

"For pretending to be a male."

"Rabette pretended to be female as well. We didn't report him for that either."

"No-genders have always been punished. Wasn't that why we were kept apart? In case we organized a rebellion?"

"Yes," Anniya admitted. "The established wisdom was that since no-genders were unable to breed, they were dispensable."

"What happened to them?" Walton asked.

"They were used as test engineers to open new seams, in medical experiments . . . Or destroyed at birth."

"Good God!"

"There were few of them left." Anniya then turned accusingly back to the Drune. "What did Pyg do to the other Ossianes?"

"Yes," joined Walton. "There must be more than two dozen of you?"

The Drune gave a sane, sinister smile. "Tell you? Then go quietly back to the gold and green?"

Rabette knew what the Drune was capable of. "But where are they?"

"Why should you worry about that now everyone realizes you're a no-gender? You do know how you'll be treated?"

"No," Anniya protested. "Things will change. They'll have to."

"If the population of Ossiane is restored they will be able to do anything they like."

A small group of inquisitive cleansing units and conversation pieces had clustered near the busy lift shaft to watch the Ossiane engineers coming and going.

"Oh well," said a small sweeper, "they seem to be sorting themselves out at last."

A greenish grey conversation piece was less sure. "That rocket started vibrations you know. They'll be an earthquake, mark my words."

This was too much for its bright orange and pink companion, which had been trying to avoid the melancholy unit's company for the last ten years. "Well you would think that wouldn't you. You said those aliens would overrun the planet but there couldn't have been more than three dozen of them. At least I now stand the chance of finding somebody to have a real conversation with."

The green unit sneered. "With you? I'll be the one in demand; always was before. These mortals revel in self-pity. They'll be queuing up to cry on my shoulder."

"Well you'd better get maintenance to fit you with a neck as well when they install them."

The discussion was beyond the cleansing units. They were unsure why they had bothered to join in. Now that none of the machinery was compelled to keep its voice down they had the uneasy sensation things were going to get out of hand; and, sure enough, the clattering of computer language was soon heard from every corner of Rosipolees. Mobile conversation pieces were demanding intelligent discussion with busy mechanics, sides of buildings and construction units. Two molecular unbonders decided to break ages of boredom by having a duel to see which could dismantle a marble pavilion the quickest. As the structure involved supported an overhead walkway and several balconies their resulting collapse attracted the attention of the city computer.

She immediately immobilized anything noisy enough to make the obsidian windows vibrate. This struck dumb most of the conversation pieces as well as grounding one or two energy unbonders and all the post wasps that had escaped from their hive.

Creaking with resignation, the cleansing units gathered up their equipment and trundled off to clear away the mess.

30

After their intolerant treatment of the Drunes, the male and female Ossianes would have been mortified to know that their existence now depended on the whim of a none-too-sane no-gender. Leaving the Ossianes' survival in the hands of Silver Ver Drene was probably down to Commander Pyg's strange sense of poetic justice.

Having learnt so much about this peculiar civilization in the crust of the Earth, Walton and Akaylia reluctantly admitted that they didn't find themselves as sympathetic to the Ossianes' plight as they might have been. Yes, they did suggest that the Drune should reinstate the lost population but, as it had so succinctly pointed out, it was hardly likely to receive the Ossiane Citizen of the Tenth Millennia Award for doing so.

And so, thinking along these lines, Walton and Akaylia found themselves standing on the balcony overlooking Rosipolees. They watched the Drune's hair glitter as it meandered into the distance, dodging the odd frantic cleansing unit and walkways full of conversation pieces waving appendages to waylay anyone or anything for a good gossip, especially about the city's computer, which was trying to improve their behaviour.

"Do you think this place could be made habitable again?" asked Walton.

Akaylia shrugged. "Plenty of our people would come down here to have a look at it, but then, we've got idiots who wouldn't mind getting onto a space shuttle."

Walton groaned. Now he was fifty, that window of opportunity was rapidly closing. "Hmmm," he pondered. "Not too sure we should say anything about this place, are you?"

"Not so sure we'd be believed, and it's going to be even more difficult to break in from now on. Anyway, you know what our lot are like. They'd probably rush in hamburger and pizza joints on every level, compel the Ossianes to accept loans that ruin the economy, then do a deal with the first dictator to muscle in when law and order breaks down. After what they've been through – assuming the Drune brings them back – they're not going to need that sort of aggravation."

"No," said Walton. "Do you think the Drune will own up to what Pyg did to the rest of the Ossianes?"

"Not sure. Depends on whether it decides to stay mad or not. I only know it might be an idea to get out of this place before it makes up its mind. You know Ossiane policy about interlopers, don't you?"

"I understand it may account for some cross breeding."

Akaylia shrugged. "Well I'm past it, but how about you, big boy?"

"God, no! I've too much alimony to pay and a beautiful, blonde wife upstairs already. My breeding days are over and I can't say I fancy going into retirement without a real garden to wander around. What good's an astronomer who can't see the sky?"

"Yes, even this geologist is beginning to find everything closing in."

"Is that what happened to the poetry?"

"The pressure must have flattened my muse."

"Good for the bones, though."

"I already have my own gravity."

Despite the attempts of the mechanic to follow her like an irritable Jack Russell terrier that had run out of things to snap at, Akaylia managed to program a capsule to take them to the entrance Walton had blundered into. Passing up through each level, they saw that machines were coming to life and buzzing around, polishing, replanting and mending as though the tourists were going to invade the next day.

As the hill had caved in, the baffled capsule wandered about for some time before coming across an alternative emergency shutter which let them out uncomfortably near Uncle Arthur's bungalow.

They looked at what was left of the hill, much of which had collapsed onto Walton's car.

"Oh bugger," he cursed. "Now we'll have to call on that old buzzard."

Akaylia knew he wasn't on about fluff and feathers as they approached the dismal farm.

Akaylia and Walton had been unable to find Rabette before they left because, now his secret was out, he had changed his tartan suit for dull overalls in the hope that when the other Ossianes came back they would not put him in a mine or turn him into the subject of a vivisection experiment. Then he followed the Drune. No longer sure about how much he hated the creature, Rabette still wanted to keep it in sight just in case he changed his mind and it disappeared forever.

Silently the engineer pursued the Drune to the far side of Rosipolees where the walkways were in a bad state of repair and conversation pieces hardly beyond alphabet level. Silver Ver Drene opened an ancient shutter and Rabette saw it enter a lobby with a lift cage. As the Drune slid open its door, Rabette called out. Silver Ver Drene turned. Rabette was the last person under Earth it expected to see. Silver Ver Drene motioned him to join it inside the cage. Rabette was used to making snap decisions, albeit the wrong ones, and quickly obeyed. The Drune showed the control its palm print and they shot upwards.

After travelling for some time the lift stopped. Silently, sullenly, the Drune beckoned him out onto a balcony. Below was a vista of walkways, gleaming meadows, fountains and the huge gem-embellished hall that Rabette had seen in the illusion conjured up by the Drune's screen. But the most remarkable thing was the sky. It was real. Cliffs rose up about the vast valley, giving it the awful stillness of a human graveyard.

Leading down into the valley was a long twisting staircase. On either side plants had got out of hand and invaded it here and there. Half way down was a large archway where two huge, sphinx-like sentinels gazed at each other across the steps.

Ignoring Rabette, the Drune wandered on ahead. Rabette followed at a distance. Knowing he wasn't going to get any answers from Silver Ver Drene he stopped by one of the sentinels. An eye opened. Rabette leapt back in alarm.

"Can I help you?" the statue asked.

Rabette could barely cope with conversation pieces. Usually they were too near his own height for comfort and there was something unsettling about facing them eyeball to proboscis. But he himself was only knee high to this entity.

"What is this place?" asked Rabette.

The sentinel slowly blinked. "This is Avacynth, the ancient refuge of the Drunes."

Rabette had always believed Avacynth to be a legend. He looked into the valley. All those sparkling walkways, fountains and the coloured obsidian, which had caught his eye, were more derelict than any city the Ossianes had inhabited.

"What happened?"

"As with most things," said the sentinel in a low humming tone, "the place eventually ran down. The Drunes weren't able to come any more. Also, we have this thing called 'weather'."

"What happened?"

"Centuries ago the Ossianes realized how intelligent the Drunes were and no longer allowed them to 'disappear'."

"You mean that they'd been living in this place for thousands of years without anyone discovering them?"

"Of course," said the sentinel. "There was no danger from any human ships."

"This is an island?"

"A volcanic island, but that was sorted out long ago. By the time humans had aircraft the place had served its purpose."

Rabette wondered whether it would be possible to send up a few cleansing units and other mechanics to sort out Avacynth? But what for? There was nobody else left to live in it. All those wonderful creatures he had seen in the Drune's screen must have been some sort of racial memory.

The sun went down so rapidly it alarmed Rabette. Lights here and there still sparkled, and dim gems of colour were dotted about the denser blackness. Silver Ver Drene could probably find its way easily enough, but Rabette made his way back to the illuminated lobby.

After some hours, Silver Ver Drene reappeared. It made for the lift, then cast a sideways glance at Rabette.

"Are you coming then?" As with Akaylia's aptitude for ghastly rhymes, its madness had disappeared.

Rabette quickly followed it into the lift and they went down to Rosipolees.

"What about the other Ossianes?" Rabette eventually asked.

The Drune gave a thin smile. "Would it be right to bring them back so we can be persecuted until the day we die?"

"But that won't happen now."

"You have been keeping yourself to yourself, haven't you, little brother."

"If you aren't willing to bring the Ossianes back, why go to such lengths to save them?"

"What about the humans and all the other creatures? Pyg would have been quite happy to let the comet slam into this planet."

Silver Ver Drene waited until they were back in Rosipolees before asking Rabette, "Do you want me to bring back the Ossianes?" It gave a wicked grin. "Shall we consult a conversation piece?"

"You've got to be joking."

The Drune went up to the nearest vase of verbal vacillation and sharply rapped its bulbous head.

It gave a bright yellow flash of surprise, then twirled its proboscis round to view the silver haired interloper. "That wasn't very polite," it announced imperiously.

"Shut up," ordered the Drune. "What mode are you plugged into?"

"What do you mean? What mode?"

"Logic or illogic?"

"I can plug into both if you want, darling."

"Trying plugging into logic without blowing a circuit."

"Oh very well." The conversation piece became less theatrical. "Go on, what do you want to discuss?"

Silver Ver Drene wandered backwards and forwards. "If you were in a large family which used and abused you, and that family was suddenly trapped at the bottom of a very deep hole – "

"Illogical," interrupted the conversation piece. "How could a whole family be stupid enough to fall down the same hole all at once?"

"Well, let's assume someone did you a favour."

"All right, but it's not logical."

"And assuming you were the only one with a rope long enough to get them out, what would you do?"

The perplexed vase bubbled up several different colours in its interior. "I'm only a conversation piece, for goodness sake. You want a mainframe computer for those sort of problems."

"Oh come on," said Rabette. "This unit needs a mechanic."

The vase flushed an annoyed raspberry red. "Well, thank you!"

But the Drune was already striding away. It should have known better than ask something with a show business complex a question like that.

Rosipolees was beginning to sparkle; the cleansing units had really oiled their wheels. Now there was no Pyg, the city could be fully illuminated. The engineers had programmed computers on other levels to refurbish and restock in preparation for the return of their inhabitants. Unfortunately, none of them had noticed the sinister sparkle in the Drune's eye.

On the balcony overlooking Rosipolees were some engineers. They had been waiting to challenge Silver Ver Drene about the location of the other Ossianes.

The Drune gazed up at the huge refrigeration palace gleaming at the centre of the city.

"Wait here," it ordered Rabette.

31

"This man makes the worst coffee I've ever tasted," whispered Akaylia, "and I've been through quite a few breakfasts."

"At least he didn't take a pot shot at us," said Walton. "I think the old boy was happy enough to see my car crushed under all those ruddy boulders. And watching that hill collapse must have cheered him up no end."

"Well, at least we managed to get out alive."

"More coffee?" demanded Uncle Arthur as he clattered about with his best enamel mugs.

"No, I'm fine," said Akaylia, hastily. "It's very good of you, but I don't suppose we could phone for a taxi?"

"Suppose so. Sure you won't have another coffee first?"

"It's just that I've got this meeting to attend." Walton cast her a dubious look. "And the Doctor here has to get back to his students."

Arthur grunted. "What? That niece of mine and her up-market friend? You ain't never gonna teach them anything. Do them good to work on a farm for a few years."

Walton glanced out of the window at the never-ending horizon of corn. If nature had any sense of justice it would have been a dust bowl years ago. No, he couldn't see Poppy and Bryony enjoying themselves here for a couple of days. They were urban hedgehogs, and he was surprised at how much he was beginning to miss the security of the garden after the last couple of days. He knew it would be months before he was able to travel on the underground without thinking about plate tectonics.

Akaylia could see that he was drifting off into a mental review of the bad dream they had just shared. She gave a warning frown and he snapped back to reality.

"Yes," said Walton, checking that his wallet hadn't been lifted by an ambitious bat. "I think a taxi's the thing."

"What's to be done about the car then?" asked Uncle Arthur. "Don't expect me to get it carted off, do you?"

"No, of course not, the insurance company will cover all that, don't you worry. Not blocking any access road, is it?"

"Well, it ain't so much the car, it's half that bloody hillside what come down on top of it."

"I see. Are you insured?" Walton asked carefully.

"Nah, don't believe in them things. 'Especially not life insurance. No way is my kith and kin gonna get money out o' my bones."

Something occurred to Akaylia. "I don't know how to put this, but the hill collapsing and all that was quite a do and the press might give it a bit of coverage . . . so I don't suppose you could forget you saw us?"

Uncle Arthur gave her an old-fashioned look. "Press? That spaceship brought the hill down ages ago, and I ain't seen hide nor hair of them since. Reckon I'm the only one what knows about it."

Akaylia said nothing. The old fellow might have been right, but it must have jogged the needle on someone's seismograph.

"Anyhow," went on Uncle Arthur. "Who am I liable to see?" He gave a knowing wink. "And, I wouldn't let on about you and your boyfriend."

Walton sighed with relief that the farmer had grasped the wrong end of the stick. He just hoped that Janice wouldn't think the same when he tried to explain where he had been. Having at last found the woman of his dreams he couldn't face another divorce before he was eighty.

While Walton and Akaylia were waiting for their respective trains they agreed, in very few words, that neither of them would speak to a living soul about the experience they had just shared some miles down in the Earth's crust. Akaylia was already regarded as a beacon for the bizarre, which constituted a threat to her department's funding, and the astronomer didn't want to end up in some UFO directory. When Walton's train arrived they exchanged cards, then nodded a swift goodbye to each other.

He was strangely relieved to get back, even to a class of art students. Teaching them astronomy no longer seemed so difficult. Compared to Pyg and the Drune they were conformity itself.

After a shower and good sleep, Akaylia rushed her satchel of samples to her laboratory. Other researchers had stopped taking her seriously ever since she ceased to look like a hippy and more like a one-woman Himalayan expedition trying to date a yeti, so they never bothered to ask where she had been.

As the geologist emptied the satchel there was a buzzing sound at the bottom of it. She rummaged about, then pulled out something that she certainly hadn't put there.

The Drune carefully guided its capsule down towards the refrigeration palace. In the back seat of the vehicle was its huge globe rippling with veins of energy. Reluctantly, Rabette and Anniya helped lift it from the capsule and seat it on its pedestal.

Rabette was beginning to feel prickles of apprehension as Silver Ver Drene sat facing the screen, gazing into its bottomless depths through half closed eyelids. The face of the ginger cat appeared. Rabette stepped back. He was sure he recognized it.

The crystal in Akaylia's hand glowed. Shaped like a dog's tooth, it was larger than the Kohinoor. Thankfully it had stopped buzzing, but she didn't want others to see her holding this strange, pulsating artifact. They knew her finds could be eccentric, but this was taking things a bit too far – nobody as yet had managed to pull a self illuminated, cut diamond from a rock seam.

Akaylia thrust the thing back into her satchel and made a hurried exit. Who could have planted the damn thing on her? Perhaps it had been one of those post wasps while her back was turned – though they wouldn't have been too bothered whether she was looking or not. Her satchel had been in Rabette's laboratory all the while so it could have been anyone. Perhaps even Rabette. Then something occurred to her. She went to the nearest phone and called Walton. Janice answered, but she wasn't curious. Numerous women from different faculties across the world were always calling him up. For some reason or other, astronomers found her husband user friendly, and she somehow sensed that Akaylia was far from blonde.

Unfortunately, Walton was in.

"Quick," said Akaylia. "Search your pockets."

"What?" said Walton.

"Search the pockets of the jacket and trousers you had on."

Walton couldn't guess what she was on about, but he went to the chair where he had carelessly thrown his jacket and riffled through the outside pockets. He pulled out a large crystal that glowed in the palm of his hand, then went back to the phone.

"Oh God," he said. "What is going on?"

"I'm not sure, but I think we're somebody's insurance policy, and it's not Uncle Arthur's."

The ginger cat on the Drune's screen faded, and in the globe's depths something sparkled.

Within the hour Akaylia and Walton were in the crystallography faculty at his college.

"Pity we can't slice the damn thing up," complained Walton.

"Don't think that would be a good move," said Akaylia.

"I've never had to analyze anything this size before."

"Hold on, I may have something that will do the job." Akaylia took a long tube from her satchel and screwed it onto a tripod.

"What's that?"

"A microscope, modified for the inspection of rocks. I used it a lot before I could recognize crystals without all the hassle – it's difficult to get a boulder under any other sort."

"Okay then, what can you see?"

Akaylia placed the lens over her crystal. It took a little while for her eyes to focus, but when they did . . .

"What's the matter? You look as though you've walked into a nasty accident.'

Akaylia backed away from the microscope so Walton could give the specimen his professional attention. "Oh, dear God!"

"As I said, insurance."

"It's not possible. Not even the Drune could do something like this."

"No, but Pyg could."

"The Drune – it knew all along. It had no intention of making a decision."

"So it left it up to us."

"That was a hell of a risk to take. What if Janice had found mine and you'd put yours through a crusher?"

"Wasn't really likely. Anyhow, now we know what do we do?" Akaylia thought for a moment. "What do these shapes remind you of, apart from teeth?"

"Well, they've been cut like gemstones, but some of the facets are quite pronounced, rather like a key. Suggests a lock of some sort?"

"Just what I was thinking and I don't have a brain wired like yours."

"You believe they must fit into something? Let's take another look. I didn't believe what I saw the first time."

But they were still there. Deep inside the crystal, a fraction of a millimetre high, were thousands and thousands of people packed side by side, frozen like plankton in a sea of ice.

"Hold on a minute. All the ones here appear to be male. What about mine?"

They examined Walton's crystal to confirm that his contained females. The scientists looked at each other. So who had the one containing the no-genders?

"The Drune?" they agreed.

The low flying, frantically whirring, striped body was probably no danger to aircraft or cats on roofs, but it scared the wits out of umpteen roosting birds and one or two late night revellers who suspected they had at last been over-taken by the DTs. Despite its allergy to water, not even a short shower was going to dampen the post wasp's pursuit of the correct address.

Janice wasn't sure why she was in the back yard, sorting the plastic, glass and paper into their respective bins at that time of night, but it seemed the only thing left to do. Walton had been good for nothing ever since he arrived back from Wonderland, or wherever the seminar on the ozone layer had been about. Perhaps he was involved in research that would enable him to write that infamous book at last. He'd always wanted to shock the world or bring down a government.

Janice was about to go back inside when there was a furious buzzing at the front door. She looked through the lattice of the side fence into the front garden and could just see the gleam of frantically beating silver wings as their owner glowered at the letterbox on the front door for refusing to accept the parcel it clutched. Janice tried to pay no attention. She didn't usually have a nip of anything to go to bed on, but as Walton was already fast asleep in the spare room with a case chained to his wrist and loaded gun under his pillow, this night had been an exception.

Janice went in the back door and peered through the letterbox. Two huge, composite eyes gave her a multiple glare back. Not knowing what induced her, she unlocked the door. The creature thrust the parcel into her hands. In the next instant the monster wasp had disappeared straight up, whirring like a circular saw. She dropped the heavy parcel. This had to be a joke thought up by Walton's students. But now, inspecting the parcel, she thought, *That's odd – no stamps!* She preferred not to thing about what she had just seen so locked the door and left the parcel on the stairs.

32

The Ossiane engineers had watched the Drune for some time. Its immobility convinced them it was up to something, but eventually they started to drift away. As they did so, a huge furious insect plunged down the lift shaft, zigzagged about the city, then went back to its hive where it switched off its wings and fell asleep with a thud.

Sure that the Ossianes had lost interest in what it was doing, Silver Ver Drene went to the refrigeration palace and pulled out a black box from a small compartment in one of its legs. It took the box to its screen and sat down once again. Checking to make sure no one else was about, not even Rabette, it looked long and hard into the globe. Very slowly, the sparkle in its depths began to take on a form. This time it was not a dragon or ginger cat, but a gleaming gem shaped rather like a dog's tooth. The Drune concentrated until it was virtually in a trance, then reached towards the screen. The image there became more and more solid until a multi-faceted jewel fell into Silver Ver Drene's hands. The Drune removed the lid of the black box and carefully pushed the gem into a slot. The globe suddenly revolved, showering Rosipolees with daggers of illumination which made the Ossiane engineers stop in their tracks. Even the conversation pieces stopped nattering.

The pulses of light hit walkways, bridges and balconies. As they did so shadowy figures formed and were instantly recognizable. Some Ossianes were alarmed while others just stood and stared in amazement at the company of Drunes taking shape.

As though having popped the last kernel of corn, the screen gradually ceased to glow and the figures scattered about the city moved. None of them showed any ill effects for their experience, in fact, none of the no-genders knew what had happened to them.

Those near the screen recognized the Ossiane Chief Technical Adviser. Soon there were two hundred or so Drunes clustered about Silver Ver Drene.

Then Anniya dashed through the throng. "Where are the others?"

Silver Ver Drene smiled. "They're safe enough."

The downfall of the Drunes' gender was probably caused by their unreasoning compassion. As some of them started to make sense of their surroundings they also wanted to know where everyone else was. Those used and abused for centuries, pleading for the return of their oppressors, made Silver Ver Drene feel guilty. But the Drune had thought about that for a long while.

It shrugged. "Commander Pyg was responsible for transforming the other Ossianes and she is no longer here."

But the Drunes were not used to inheriting empires; they had always lived their lives in the niches other people had allowed them to occupy. What could they do with an empire of underground cities? They couldn't reproduce and people them.

Silver Ver Drene remained inscrutable. It had sent the keys containing the other Ossianes far enough away in the hope it could not be persuaded to restore them. It left the remonstrating Drunes and gossiping conversation pieces to go and think in Pyg's dimly lit control chamber. If only it had a mind like hers the decision would be no problem.

Silver Ver Drene eventually decided to ask Rosipolees' computer for a chat.

It was just as well the post wasp did not return to Walton's address the following morning. If he hadn't shot it on sight, Janice would have set about it with her two-iron.

Akaylia was already slipping back into her live-and-let-live mode, and wasn't too worried about the arrival of the second furious giant wasp through the open window of her flat. Cats spat, dogs howled on balconies and a neighbour screamed as it flew through her washing, but they were all sounds common to the neighbourhood. As she swallowed her morning rum baba, Akaylia read the Drune's letter. Walton was going to be relieved that it had made up its mind.

Akaylia and Walton watched as two post wasps zoomed out of a volcanic fumarole. They approached their outstretched hands, snatched up the packages containing the gems and black boxes and disappeared back down the vent.

"Right, now that's all over let's get back before your wife starts thinking you've changed your taste in women."

Walton hesitated to muse, "Isn't it odd."

"What is?"

"The species who become extinct are usually the ones who have the most compassion."

Akaylia paused. "Not really. You're not thinking of turning into a Drune as a politically correct statement, are you? I understand the operation is irreversible."

Walton quickly shrugged off the idea, then followed the geologist knowing that, one way or the other, he was going to have nightmares for the rest of his life.

First, Silver Ver Drene placed the female Ossianes' crystal in its slot. The screen changed, with a huge flash of light that struck terror into the conversation pieces whose mood swings were controlled by subtle changes in illumination. Thousands and thousands of females were restored wherever the darts struck. The Drunes dashed about Rosipolees, trying to help re-orientate the Ossianes, but as they were prohibited from touching them the process was more of an exercise in trying to show they were blameless for what had happened.

Once they had been persuaded to take cover, Silver Ver Drene took up the remaining crystal and restored the male Ossianes. By the time it had finished, the city was a crowded place, and the lifts worked to their limit, ferrying citizens up to their respective levels. Through it all, their Chief Technical Adviser sat pondering whether it should have flown away with Pyg. The premonition of what was about to come made the Ealinans seem quite cuddly.

The Ossiane engineers did their best to explain what had happened but, whatever they said or proof they produced, the ruling council remained convinced that Silver Ver Drene had been the tool through which some monstrous alien had taken control of their empire. Any other explanation was inconceivable to a decadent species, which had spent ten millennia underground. Someone had to take the blame. Their Chief Technical Adviser had been imprisoned because they believed it had become unstable and dangerous. Only a force for evil would have released it.

When Anniya arrived in Rosipolees to warn Silver Ver Drene that the council had decided to liquidate all the Drunes, it was sitting on the remains of its crystal prison as though it were a throne. The city was quite deserted, with not even the sound of a conversation piece clearing its throat. The Drune turned to look at the engineer and gave a strangely warm smile.

"What happened?" asked Anniya. "Where are the cleansing units and conversation pieces?" She saw half a dozen ancient androids scurrying to the far side of the city with large pieces of equipment, the Drune's screen and cases of food. She knew it wasn't for a picnic. "Where's Rabette?" she asked apprehensively.

"Safe, as long as you immobilize all the lift cages after you've reached the next level."

Anniya hesitated. "Why?"

"It will save me time."

Two more androids creaked with centuries of inactivity as they strode across to the far side of Rosipolees.

"But they've got the city computer's main memory? And how did you get those ancient androids back into commission?"

"I was saving them for a rainy day."

"Rain?"

"They were the only waterproof models."

"What's rain?"

"Living with Pyg for so long taught me the value of insurance."

All Ossianes knew what that was. Anniya raised her eyebrows. "Whatever you're up to, you'd better be quick about it. The council ordered us to renovate an army of soldier robots to round up the Drunes."

"Would you like to find out what rain is, Anniya?"

Anniya was tempted but, unlike Rabette, never made snap decisions about her own survival. "I'll immobilize the lift. Is this level clear?"

"Yes." Silver Ver Drene rose rather dreamily.

"Good luck!" Anniya scuttled back to the lift.

When she reached the next level she blew out the circuits operating the cages. The Drune sealed the shaft by bringing across a series of bulkhead shutters. As it did so sirens on every level wailed alarm at the prospect of pressure failure, but the soldier robots were already on the move. They were like a cross between a jackknife and lobster, and were also waterproof. They had entered Rosipolees through the lake where the emergency shutters took longer to close.

Before Silver Ver Drene could make it to the lift the clanking army had cut off its escape. Seconds to detonation ticked by as it ducked, leapt, swerved and even swam to avoid the lumbering units. It was too late to curse itself for not destroying the robots when it had the chance and any weapons Silver Ver Drene could get into the lift were now above in Avacynth, with people of its own kind who had no idea how to use them.

Hurtling through several panes of coloured obsidian, the Drune fell straight into the crushing clutches of a robot. Time was running out. Within minutes the ancient city would implode and be claimed back into the mantle.

Robots did not possess the subtle natures of androids. When programmed to hold onto something, no intellectual argument would persuade them to let go.

Barely conscious, the Drune glimpsed a sudden flash of light. One of the robots fell in a fountain of sparks, which fortunately didn't ignite the oxygen rich atmosphere, and their loop command was momentarily confused. Silver Ver Drene struggled free and dashed towards its rescuer. With only forty seconds left, whoever was in that pressure suit had to get them to the lift or be vaporized in a cauldron of molten iron.

The robots quickly restored their chain of command and kept coming.

President Glutt and the ruling council in Chippertii several levels above watched the pictures relayed from cameras in the robot's helmets as their Chief Technical Adviser was half dragged into a secret lift by a creature three-quarters its size. That was the last they saw of Silver Ver Drene. The leading robot held onto the underside of the lift, but the cage accelerated so rapidly the machine lost its grip and smashed on the shaft's floor.

There was a dull thud from the bottom of Rosipolees' test shaft and a series of fractures rapidly radiated away from it. Obsidian walls that had stood since the time of the ancients, hiding the desiccated corpses of the city's last plague, cracked as the pressure increased. Rosipolees' massive shielding began to buckle, unable to breach the puncture made by the explosion.

Pyg's complex was first to disappear. Then the ceiling of Rosipolees bellied downwards, its buttresses screeching under the strain of supporting several miles of rock and iron. The molecules maintaining the shield's rigidity boiled and the concretion ran away in molten rivers. Every level above shook. Unable to stand, the Ossianes rolled into quake shelters as buildings toppled about them and surface cracks appeared in shield walls. It was some time before the movement stopped. Though dented, the cities above remained intact. Never in living memory had the Ossianes needed to cope with a collapse on that scale, and the only person who knew how to prevent it happening again was last seen disappearing upwards in a secret lift. Perhaps liquidating the more intelligent Drunes had not been such a good idea after all. Ossiane civilization had only survived comfortably because they had been such compliant problem solvers, now some alien had taught one of them to know better and emptied the pepper pot into their ambrosia.

Silver Ver Drene shielded its eyes from the sun as it tumbled from the lift lobby. In the fierce daylight it could now see its rescuer clutching a helmet and a welding blaster with the confidence of a buttress engineer.

"Rabette . . ."

"So?"

"I didn't think you could handle a weapon?"

"Nor did I until I'd spent time trying to motivate these Drunes. I'm not surprised they were almost wiped out."

The Drune looked down into the valley where the rescued conversation pieces were chatting to Avacynth's new inhabitants. It could see what Rabette meant. They may have been safe from the Ossianes but wouldn't have stood a chance against a flock of marauding seagulls.

Rabette followed Silver Ver Drene. "They reckon they can't cope with living outside. Want to know if it's possible to give the place a lid?"

"Yes," said Silver Ver Drene absently. Having reached the valley floor it wandered amongst the derelict buildings. "We have to start repairing and planting first."

The Drunes watched their leader in bland acquiescence. Some made token attempts to lift wall frames back into place and pull the occasional weed.

Unable to walk any further, Silver Ver Drene leaned against the nearest thing that would take its weight. Unfortunately that was a conversation piece.

Its bell-like body flushed with empathy. "Let me say on behalf of all the cleansing units, post wasps, errand moles, molecular unbonders and conversation pieces – " An irritated bleep at plinth level interrupted it. "And, of course – MECHANICS – how grateful we all are for – "

"Shut up," said the Drune. "Just remember what I brought you up here for."

"Now, we conversation pieces wanted to talk to you about that."

"Just do as you've been programmed."

"But really, we were never designed to talk about . . ."

"About what?" asked Rabette.

"You know. Digging, building common hovels, laying pathways – SEWERS!"

As its strength returned, Silver Ver Drene was getting annoyed. "We don't have enough androids, but we've got two hundred Drunes who need to be occupied. If they want to live up here, you are going to have to tell them how."

"But surely they'll listen to you?"

"Oh, no!" The Drune backed away towards a bland building with no windows. It keyed in a security code and the shutters swung open. After feeding the doorpost's computer with several more instructions, a long cigar shaped vessel floated from the shelter. A hatch opened and the Drune stepped inside to check a bank of controls.

"You're not . . ." Rabette started apprehensively, pointing to the sky, ". . . not going up there, are you?"

"Why not?"

"You're bailing out on us, aren't you?"

Though not true, Silver Ver Drene was put out by the accusation. "What if I am?"

"Then take me with you."

"You're needed here."

Rabette hurled down his helmet and it bounced off a nearby conversation piece. "How long do you think I can stay on an island filled with this mildew-brained circus?"

The conversation piece flushed in annoyance. "Oh really, that's strong coming from a milky Munchkin like you."

Rabette recognized Akaylia's tone in its words. He raised the welding blaster and singed its proboscis. It screeched.

Silver Ver Drene could see he was angry enough to thumb a lift from a passing whale. "But I need you, Rabette. Don't blame the others for the way they've been conditioned. It will take time to bring them round. Weren't we both like that at one time?"

"I doubt it," snapped Rabette.

"Of course, you always wanted to be human, didn't you?"

Rabette indicated the cigar shaped vessel. "How far can that thing travel?"

Suddenly a post wasp zipped erratically in from nowhere, whirring with annoyance at what the damp salt air had done to its circuits, scowled at the Drune, then disappeared into its makeshift hive.

In Chippertii, President Glutt, leader of the Ossiane high council, waited for his alabaster chair of office to be righted before sitting down to read out the letter to the shaken members of the ruling elite.

> *To all Ossiane true Born, greetings from one of the third condition . . .*

The correct formal address was reassuring, but if the Chief Technical Adviser was about to ask for its position back the price was going to be a high one. Already the members were discussing the aspirations they had for it to create them a new technology, far in advance of anything the humans above had.

President Glutt called them to order, then read on:

> *I should regret the action it was necessary to take to preserve the small handful of surviving Drunes, but I don't. After all, you were going to exterminate us.*

A surge of anger rumbled about the chamber.

> *Perhaps it would be best if no more Drunes were born?*

The annoyance turned to interest.

I had time to locate the source of all the rivers supplying your reservoirs. Every so often a chemical will be tipped into each and ensure that no Ossiane female can give birth to a Drune.

A murmur of approval arose, but President Glutt had not finished the letter.

It will also ensure that no female or male Ossianes are born. As this will give you some incentive to ponder on extinction, you might also like to think about how much a prejudice is worth?

*

Akaylia stopped chipping at the basalt to admire the view below. Bobbing towards her through the long grass was a mop of white hair, this time its owner was carrying a large Ossiane suitcase.

FRANK RYAN

THE SUNDERED WORLD

Book One of the Epic Fantasy Series by International Best-Selling Author

In the violent streets of a pre-apocalyptic London, Alan Duval is wounded by the poisoned blade of a ceremonial dagger. His life is saved by a mysterious feral girl. Then, suddenly, bewilderingly, he is transported from Earth to Tír, a strange land of magic and wonder, where he is given the powers of the Oraculum of the terrible Trídédana. So begins the epic fantasy in which Duval begins a great river journey through a spectacular wilderness dominated by the forces of good and evil . . .

ISBN 1-874082-24-3 £6.99

Available through your bookseller or post-free from Swift Publishers by direct mail or order through our website:
www.swiftpublishers.com

SEAN WILLIAMS

METAL FATIGUE

Winner of the Aurealis Award for Best Science Fiction Novel

In a dystopic world after a devastating world war, the American city of Kennedy has walled itself off from the decline of the former USA. Determined to continue as a functioning metropolis, Kennedy strictly patrols its boundaries and struggles to maintain the semblance of a modern city. But now, forty years after the war, Kennedy is in crisis. Technologies are failing and replacements and repairs are not forthcoming. It is within this atmosphere of technological and social stagnation that a new and terrible danger arrives as news of a Re-United States of America emerges and a RUSA that insists that Kennedy rejoin . . .

ISBN 1-874082-29-4 £16.99

Available through your bookseller or post-free from Swift Publishers by direct mail or order through our website:
www.swiftpublishers.com

From the International Best-Selling Author

FRANK RYAN

THE THRILLER TRILOGY

ISBN 1-874082-26X

£6.99

ISBN 1-874082-01-4

£5.99

ISBN 1-874082-25-1

£6.99

Described as "Magnificently tense" in a Sunday Times review, or "simply unputdownable" by media readers such as Tony Capstick and Ashley Franklin, each book is a complete thriller in itself but they are interlinked by plot and the life of the investigating detective, Sandy Woodings. Try one and you are unliklely to resist the temptation to read them all.

Available through your bookseller or post-free from Swift Publishers by direct mail or order through our website:
www.swiftpublishers.com